our secret, siri aang

Three very special people helped me with this book. As always, thanks to my husband, Joe, for his support and encouragement. Also, a very big thanks to Patricia Lee Gauch, my editor extraordinaire, who inspired me to write the best that I can. And a very special thanks to Kakuta Ole Maimai Hamisi, who read my manuscript (more than once) for cultural accuracy, contributed invaluable cultural insights into the Maasai culture, provided translations and has become a very good friend. *Ashe* to each one of you.

our secret, siri aang

CRISTINA KESSLER

Philomel Books • New York

Patricia Lee Gauch, editor

Published simultaneously in Canada.
Printed in the United States of America.
Designed by Semadar Megged.   Text set in 11.5-point Berling.

Library of Congress Cataloging-in-Publication Data
Kessler, Cristina.   Our secret, Siri Aang / Cristina Kessler.   p. cm.
Summary: Namelok, a Masai girl, tries to persuade her traditionalist father to
delay her initiation and marriage because they will restrict her freedom and keep
her from the black rhino mother and baby she is protecting from poachers.
[1. Masai (African people)—Fiction. 2. Sex role—Fiction. 3. Culture conflict—
Fiction. 4. Black rhinoceros—Fiction. 5. Rhinoceroses—Fiction. 6. Poaching—
Fiction. 7. Kenya—Fiction.] I. Title.
PZ7.K4824Ou 2004   [Fic]—dc22   2003024075
ISBN 0-399-23985-5
1 3 5 7 9 10 8 6 4 2
First Impression

Prologue

HER STOMACH WAS huge, and it was obvious she would soon give birth. With deliberate, small steps that seemed impossible given her size, she walked slowly through the deep bush. Holding her head high, she looked left and right, and smelled the air for signs of danger, looking for a safe place to have her baby.

The heat hummed with the constant buzz of countless cicadas, and the hot, dry air hung like a heavy blanket across her back. Her slow progress filled the air, and dry branches crunched beneath her feet as she forced her way through the dense thicket. Scrubby trees with brittle branches like pointed fingers grew low to the ground and snapped as she pushed her way into the thick, crisscrossing mass. Thistle bushes dropped puddles of their nasty cram-crams, little balls of pointed needles that clamp onto skin. They collected on her rough hide, but that didn't faze her even slightly in her search.

She stopped suddenly, listening to the barks of grazing and frolicking zebra on the open plain behind her dense copse of bush. Listening carefully, she heard another series of breaking branches, snaps filling the air. It was to her west, where the sun was now tipping toward the horizon. Her eyes, good for seeing only short distances, could just make out a tall, upright shape skirting the edge of her surrounding bush. She wanted to leave, and she wanted to charge, but she knew she could do neither, for her time was at hand.

1

NAMELOK ALWAYS SAVORED her early afternoons when she went in search of firewood. Each day she wandered farther, knowing the dangers that could lie in wait, but always lured on by the calls of the birds singing a dozen different songs, by the possible natural secrets hiding behind the next small hill or clump of acacia trees. She loved her freedom and the distance between her and all others, especially in these days when dissension between young and old ruled the home *enkangs*.

She loved the sounds of the bush. The low sweet throb of mourning doves calling *work harder—work har- rrrddddderrr*, the screeching of guinea fowl, and the comforting *whish* of wings as a flock of egrets passed overhead. The constant buzz of the cicadas made her feel safe, for they only stopped when danger was near.

Her slender neck was covered in a bead choker of many colors. Red, blue, green and white symbolizing the things most important to her Maasai culture—blood, sky, good pastures and milk. A layer of three large, stiff beaded necklaces, each bigger than the one before, circled her neck and softly clicked together on her shoulders as she wandered along the outside border of the dense growth of acacia trees. Her long dangling earrings made of beaded hide sometimes caught on her necklaces as she stooped and bent to collect her wood. She was glad of the gentle *slap, slap* from her leather sandals, for the ground was thick with giant nasty thorns protruding from fallen branches, strewn across the path. All the dead wood lying about was a treasure trove.

Stopping at a pile that she had already made, she bent to grab a branch too long to carry on her back. With a swift snatch she picked it up, the longest in the pile, stepped on it in the middle and pulled the end up, snapping it in two.

Humming to herself, she worked her way slowly but noisily around the copse of dense brush. "If no one else knows of this place, then I can come every day for months, the wood is so plentiful," she said to her shadow splayed across the trees. She laughed aloud at the thought of her mother, who had told Namelok more than once that talking to oneself was not a good thing.

"Only old crones and people not quite right in the head speak in conversations of one," her mother had scolded her just that morning. "Talk to me. Talk to your father. Talk to your three sisters, or your siblings from your father's other wives—but do not talk to yourself."

Out in the bush she was free to converse with herself, or the trees, or the dipping hornbills as they flew overhead. "Free!" she called out to the herd of graceful Thompson gazelles grazing nearby. So caught up was she with her mumbling and chuckling that she didn't know when the silence she suddenly noticed had actually begun. Not a cicada was buzzing, and even the birds seemed to be holding their breaths. Cocking her head to one side to listen, she began a slow but penetrating look into the tangle of limbs and bushes. That's when she saw it, a dark mound deep in the bush.

Namelok watched as the black mound moved its head back and forth, its quivering nostrils sucking in the air and foreign scent while its ears flicked independently from front to back, listening in all directions. Its sides bulged, and with a sudden puffing snort, it kicked away a few large branches, then dropped to the earth, its breathing rapid and ragged. Its sides heaved.

The young Maasai girl froze, then whispered with complete awe, *Emuny Narok*—a black rhino. Father had taught her about each animal before letting her go into the bush alone. Now she tried to focus on his words of the past, rather than the angry ones he would voice if he knew how far she had wandered from the family's *enkang.* "Namelok-ai," he had said long ago, "each animal must be met differently. Never run from the elephant, just freeze. And if you meet the hippo, climb up a tree or rock."

"I know that he respects all animals in the wild, and reveres the cow, but what did he tell me about the black rhino?" she whispered under her breath. Namelok thought hard as she watched the bulging beast that was making no move toward her, or away. When it dropped to the ground, the girl smiled widely as she realized what was going on. In a voice loud enough for the struggling rhino to hear her she said, "Push, mother. Push hard!"

Then she remembered the encouraging sounds her father always gave his she-cows giving birth, and from a place she didn't know inside herself, out rolled a long deep sound, something she had never uttered before, "Currrr currrr," which made the mother relax. They both took a deep breath, and her father's words about the rhino came to her. "The white ones," he had said, "are larger and calmer, with big heads close to the ground for grazing. They live together, like our family groups. The black rhinos are smaller and fierce, and live alone in the bush. Their heads are smaller, far off the ground. Like its cousin the white rhino, it is nearly blind, but the black rhino is always ready to attack, so they are the ones to worry about."

"Not this one," Namelok said to the bush as the cicadas began to buzz once again and birdcalls filled in the silence. A loud grunt, almost like the puffing snort that precedes a charge, came from the struggling female. The rhino, whose ears could hear danger at a long distance, dropped her head to the ground. If the low murmur she had heard a moment before was dangerous, so be it. The labor pains were coming quickly in a rapid series of contractions. All of the rhino's attention was focused on getting the birth over with as quickly as possible. She knew she was in great danger during the process.

"Push, mother," the young girl called, a little louder this time. "Push harder. I'll watch for the lion," she tried to reassure her. She didn't know if it was her imagination, but it seemed like the rhino relaxed a degree, her head resting on the ground.

"Push," Namelok called again. She had seen her father and brothers help the she-cows in their herd give birth. She had even helped her father's third wife, Nasieku, give birth to her newest half sister, still to be named. Remembering the experience clearly, she called again, "Push harder," hoping her voice floating across the hot African afternoon would help.

With a push that Namelok nearly felt from afar, a small black head popped out from the panting mother's birth canal. It glistened in the sunlight, slick with mucus. Another loud groan and giant push produced the front legs, held together like the tightly tied legs of a calf waiting to be branded. One more push and out popped the rest of the tiny black animal, lying on the ground like a sopping pile of laundry.

The mother rhino took a deep breath, then jumped to her feet and whirled around to her freshly born baby. Taking one quick look in all directions, lingering for a split second on the tall shape in the distance, the mother rhino licked her baby clean. As she swiped at the gooey calf with long tongue strokes, it struggled to stand, its little legs, not a minute old, churning the air as it tried to rise. With a concentration as intense as Namelok had ever seen, the mother continued cleaning her baby, gently encouraging it to lie still for a few moments. When the mucus and blood were gone, the mother tenderly rubbed her nose along her baby's body, then with her head carefully nudged it until the baby stood on its four wobbly legs.

"She's beautiful," called Namelok. The rhino clearly heard the voice, but gave no sign of fright. It was as if a silent agreement had been made in the late-afternoon African bush between the Maasai girl and the rhino. Encouraged, Namelok called again, "I am Namelok-ai, the name my father gave me. It means My Sweetest One. You I shall call *Yieyio* Emuny Narok, Mother Black Rhino, and let's call your beautiful baby Siri Aang, for that's what she shall be—Our Secret."

NAMELOK HEARD THE voices as she neared the *enkang*. Afraid that it was going to be another angry night at home, she checked her shadow to see if she was late and possibly responsible for the noise. With relief she noticed that her shadow fell on the ground only as long as she was tall, meaning it was still hours from sunset. Experience had taught her that a long shadow meant many problems.

She was so excited by her rhino experience, she feared everyone she met would notice and demand to know where she had been. Her heart raced in her chest, and she was sure that her ring of necklaces was bouncing quickly with her heartbeats. She stopped to calm herself and said under her breath, "This is a secret, one I will share with no one. Not even with Father." Then she blurted out, "Why did I bring so much wood?" She knew the heavy pile on her back could last two or three days. "Dumb," she scolded herself. "I don't want to wait that long to visit the rhinos again."

So caught up was she in her conversation of one that Namelok was surprised by an old grandmother suddenly standing before her. Namelok dropped her stack of firewood and dipped her head in respect. The old woman placed her hand upon the girl's head in greeting and said, "Namelok-ai, *supa!*"

"Good afternoon, *Kokooo*," Namelok said, using the respectful name of Grandmother to the old woman who was no relation. She was certain that her excitement from the afternoon was written across her face, so she said quickly, "Are you well, Grandmother?"

The woman blessed her and said, "It is time for a Naming Ceremony. Nasieku's newest born will be named tomorrow, so there is much to prepare. I am going now to tell the other *enkangs*." With that, the woman, bent by age, scurried away to spread the good news of the upcoming ceremony.

With her heart still pounding in her chest like stampeding buffalo, Namelok entered the family *enkang* through the gatepost facing north in the wall of piled branches surrounding the huts. Inside, in front of the huts, was another large circle, enclosed by another fence made of branches from four different types of trees. Prominent large thorns stood out every which way. The circles of branch fences kept predators from leaping inside to kill the livestock that also lived inside the *enkang*. She looked at the five rounded, squat huts behind the empty animal circle.

Two huts stood to the left and three to the right on either side of the main entrance in the thorn wall. They were very short and made from mud and cow dung, sticks and urine, even bits of grass. She looked at the first hut on the left, the hut her mother had built and shared with her two youngest daughters and sometimes with her husband, Reteti, but there was no one there. Next Namelok looked at the dormitory hut where she slept with her sister and three other girls from her age group. No one was there either.

Then she glanced next door at the hut of wife number four and saw her father's newest wife, nearly her own age, duck inside. The new wife was unhappy about being married to such an old man, even though tradition said a girl will marry a man at least twice her age. Everyone knew of her unhappiness, and Namelok was insulted. All who knew her father, Reteti, knew he was an exceptional man.

Namelok turned to the right side of the compound as a flow of women erupted from the first wife's hut, like an anthill spewing out its inhabitants, as they all followed Nanana out of her hut. The women chattering reminded Namelok of the busy community of weaver birds just outside the *enkang*. She loved to do her beadwork near the nests, for the constant activity of the little weavers with their white heads, brown backs and red rumps entertained her. They flitted about their nests, scolding one another with incessant chattering notes, just like the women emerging from the hut.

Her mother, Namunyak, smiled when she saw her daughter. She crossed the compound and Namelok dropped her head in greeting. Her mother tenderly touched it, and then said, "My Sweetest One, you look very excited. Is there news for me?"

"News?" she asked, knowing that her mother wanted to know if her monthly bleeding had begun yet. It was a question she had recently begun asking daily. "No, no news," she answered, savoring the real news, the secret of beautiful little Siri Aang out in the bush.

Her mother said, "You have been gone a long while. I hope you are not going too far, for there are many dangerous animals out there, especially in the dry season. The younger herd boys returned with news of fresh lion spoor, not far from the water hole."

"That should make the warriors happy," said Namelok. "Will all the Elders allow them to hunt it?"

Namelok thought about all the problems in their new village of family *enkangs*. Some of the Elders, like her father and all the older generations, were resisting the changes being forced upon them. For as long as these older men and women could remember, the test of manhood for a young warrior was to kill a lion with a spear. Sometimes a warrior killed a lion alone, not planning the attack because it happened on the spur of the moment while he grazed his herd. Planned group hunts were something else. Particularly now, since the Kenyan government had banned lion hunting, planned hunts were usually arranged in secret.

Tapping her thighs with both fists balled, Namelok said, "Do you think the Junior Elders will agree to a lion hunt? Especially Saitoti, the one who makes Father so angry?" Namelok knew from listening that he was a Junior Elder who agreed to banning hunts to please the government.

Namunyak nodded her head. "Not to worry, my Sweetest One, there will be a lion hunt, of that I am sure." She gazed across the compound in thought. "Our warriors are compelled to hunt down any lion that threatens us or our animals. Every Elder, young or old, knows this and will agree to a hunt."

"I wish Loitipitip was here," Namelok said to her mother. She and her oldest half brother had spent years together herding sheep and goats in the bush, off for the whole day by themselves. "He is very brave." She remembered the time she had squatted behind a termite hill to relieve herself when Loitipitip suddenly came running, screaming at the top of his lungs and throwing rocks as he ran. Namelok still could feel the lurch of her heart as she relived the shock of turning and seeing an ugly old hyena change its course and run from her rather than at her. It had been close enough for her to see the gleam of its yellow eyes and the large fang teeth that filled its mouth. When she turned to her brother, they both knew that Loitipitip had just saved Namelok's life, and their bond was even stronger. "Loitipitip would go after this lion alone, for he is fearless," Namelok said. "Just think, *Yieyio*, how handsome he would look in a lion's-mane headdress."

Namunyak took her daughter's hand, and the two joined the group of women who were still talking excitedly. The older women had closely shaven heads, with beaded bands around where their hairlines used to be. Nanana wore the most jewelry as a symbol of her wealth and stature in the household as first wife. Long dangling strings of red and white beads hung from holes in the tops of her ears, and her droopy earflaps of skin supported metal triangles. Her cow-skin dress hung nearly to the ground, with piles of bead necklaces draped down her flattened breasts. All listened when she spoke, including Namelok.

Pointing at the women one by one, or in groups of two or three, she made assignments for the Baby Naming Ceremony. "You will bring the sacrificial goat," she told Namelok's mother. Then, pointing at her two oldest daughters, she said, "You will bring the honey beer for the Elders after the ceremony." Tapping her flat chest, she said, "I will be responsible for the killing and roasting of the goat."

Nasieku, so proud of her beautiful baby, sat in the shade of her hut, listening to her two older co-wives as they planned her daughter's Naming Ceremony. Again and again she lifted her child high, blowing on her belly, just below the beaded waistband. Namelok watched them, and smiled as a tiny little giggle flowed from the happy baby's mouth.

When Nanana spotted the pile of firewood that Namelok had just brought in, she said, "That is a good beginning, Namelok. Can you bring more tomorrow morning, early?"

Namelok was quick to reply, "Yes, Nanana, it would be my honor." Trying not to look too happy about extra work, she glowed inside. This gave her an excuse to visit the rhinos the very next day. She would make sure that no harm had come to the baby rhino. And she would see if the mother would still allow her presence. Namelok knew that just because Emuny Narok accepted her today didn't mean she would automatically let her come near them again. More than once her father had talked of the dangerous black rhino, warning that "Man is the rhino's worst enemy. Ignorant people kill them for their horns, and in turn the rhinos kill people that come too close. And who can blame them?" he finished each time, which made Namelok love him even more now.

Namelok thought of these words now and wondered out loud, "Shall I die trying to get too close?" She didn't have a long time to reflect on it, for her mother clapped her hands and said, "Are you speaking to us? Or is it a conversation of one in public?" There was no smile on her mother's face. Namelok regretted speaking out loud, but the question did not go away.

She was glad when the herd of cows returned, for her mother forgot about her as everyone gathered at the main gate to welcome the animals back. "You are so beautiful," sang one of the herders as the animals poured into the inner circle that provided them safety at night. Namelok looked across the high backs of the cows as they came in, and saw her father through the cloud of dust stirred up by the animals' feet. She always looked forward to seeing him at the end of the day.

Namelok thought about how her father had changed since they had moved to this new area. Being driven years ago from much of his traditional place by a loss of grazing lands to a big nature reserve, and now losing more to encroaching wheat farmers, had made her father an angry man. He fought tenaciously to hang on to his Maasai ways. His face used to be peaceful and happy—she could still see it in her mind's eye. Now he usually wore a frown that looked as though a passing cloud had swallowed his heart. Even in his new angry mood she loved him fiercely, for he was the brightest, bravest and kindest man she knew.

Namelok bowed her head across the brown and white and black backs of the passing cows, and was relieved to see her father smile back at her. She knew this was his favorite time of day, for he was happy to see his family of four wives and fifteen of his sixteen children showing the respect he demanded for his cattle by gathering to welcome them home each night.

"It is such a simple gesture," he had told the family when they were settled in their new *enkang*. "We are in a new place, and there are many things that are not the same, but this will stay the same, my children. Each night we will follow the tradition of welcoming the herd and thanking Enkai, creator of all cattle, for giving the Maasai all of her cattle."

All knew of his disgust for the families that were forgetting to observe even this old tradition. "We shall do it every night," her father, Reteti, insisted. Because he was the undisputed head of his *enkang*, no one dared disagree, but in truth all in Reteti's family enjoyed it. To Namelok it meant it was nearly the end of the workday and the beginning of the social evening.

Once the cows were enclosed, everyone moved about their last business, enjoying a break from the sun's punishing heat. Namelok went quickly to her mother's hut for the milk-gourd cleaning tools. The two special sticks she needed were stored under the bed, and the gourds rested in a neat pile on the right side of the bed. Cleaning the gourds was a job she had been doing since she was old enough to help with the herds. Grabbing everything she needed, she stepped back out into the softening dusky light.

As she stirred the fire, she could only think about the baby rhino out in the bush. "Tomorrow cannot come too soon," she whispered to the calves, who called out to their mothers returning from a day of grazing. Long low moos filled the air as the mother cows called back to their babies. In the dust across the compound Namunyak placed the gate back in the cattle entrance, then looked to see if her daughter was ready with the clean gourds so she could milk the cows.

Namelok bent close to the fire and selected a stick of *oloirien* with a flaming red ember at its end. She broke glowing red pieces of burning charcoals off into the top of the milk gourd, then quickly shook it back and forth so the flame would die inside the gourd. Her grandmother had taught her the secrets of cleaning gourds, and to always be sure that it was done right, for if not, many would fall ill. Namelok rested the soft handle of the olive wood *oloirien* next to the fire, to save for another cleaning. Humming as she worked, she picked up another tool, a stick with a bent top and a fluff of fibers sticking out the top. She stuck the *esosian* stick inside the gourd and rubbed it around, cleaning the inside walls with the ash of the hot coals she had dropped into the gourd, killing all bacteria inside.

Her mother watched her daughter's efficient hands and said, "Finish with that gourd so I can start milking. I like to watch you work, for you show the experience of one who has done this many times. You're really a grown-up girl, My Sweetest One."

Namelok dropped her head and smiled to herself at her mother's rare compliment. Bending over a small bowl, she tapped out the ash. With a swift motion she picked up the cleaning stick, curved with a cow's-tail whisk attached at the end. She rammed it into the gourd and swished it around, clearing all lingering ash from inside.

With pride she handed it to her mother and said, "Here, *Yieyio-ai*, the cleanest milk gourd in the *enkang*."

Her mother gave a little snort and said, "Please go fry the meat for dinner, for the herd boys are hungry. Your sister can clean the other two gourds." As she grabbed the teats on the heavy udder of her favorite cow, her mother said, "Remember, a little modesty is not a bad thing."

chapter
3

As DARKNESS OVERTOOK the massive sky, loud voices filled the *enkang*. Tomorrow was a big day, for the warriors would go on a lion hunt and her father's newest baby would be named.

"There is no choice," said Namelok's father to the group of Elders sitting with him under the giant baobab tree. Namelok hung back in the shadows with the group that had gathered to listen. "This lion must be hunted." Reteti sucked his teeth and looked directly at Saitoti, who argued almost daily with him that the government was right to ban lion hunts. "And what do you say, Mr. Voice of the Government? Shall they hunt the lion that is menacing our herd or not?"

All eyes rested on the young man who had angered the Elders more than once. He tapped the ground with his *oringa* stick with the beautiful beaded handle his mother had made for him. His eyes met Reteti's across the campfire as he sucked his lips into a narrow angry line, and looking around at all who watched him closely, Saitoti said, "I am not the voice of the government." He cleared his throat and focused on Reteti. "I know when a lion must be hunted, and that time is now." He rose from the ground and said to one and all, "I am not your enemy. Don't think that I am not Maasai because I look to the future." He twirled his *oringa* to take in everyone, including Namelok and the other listeners who had gathered. "I vote yes, the *ilmurani* must hunt this lion." Then he clicked his tongue against the roof of his mouth and stalked off.

Reteti completely ignored his departure as he pointed his fly whisk at the remaining men. *Aaa*'s of agreement flowed from mouth to mouth like water over rocks in a riverbed. At last the final Elder, the *Loibon* holy man for the group, sighed out a long "*Aaa*, yes," then said, "I bless the *ilmurani* warriors who will hunt tomorrow. May their nerves be strong and their spears fly straight as they hunt the dangerous lion." He scratched the sparse gray whiskers that dotted his cheeks and chin, and said, "So be it. The lion hunt begins tomorrow." Namelok shuddered.

A young warrior burst from the group of listeners and ran to the separate *manyatta* where the warriors lived. Whoops of happiness filled the air as the high-pitched voice of a younger warrior sang a song to give courage to the hunting party of the oldest and bravest. A deep, harmonious chorus of voices resonated across the savannah, "An-ya-ha, an-ya-ha," filling all hearts with pride as the young man, his voice high and clear above all the others, sang,

"Our fearless warriors, brave and true,
trained like the sharp edges of our swords,
fast like the cheetah,
will start the hunt with the rising sun.

Oh, lion, may a pointed spear
pierce your heart
and keep our families and cattle safe.
You are no match for our fearless warriors."

The clang of cowbells mixed with the bellows of feisty bulls and singing voices. As the moon rose, the shouts of children playing lion hunt died down, and their mothers chased them into their huts to sleep. The conversations subsided, but the deep humming voices of the singing warriors, "An-ya-ha, an-ya-ha, an-ya-ha," accompanied the cicadas long into the night.

Lying on her bed with her sister Lankat pressed against her, Namelok jerked from the edge of sleep. "Please, Enkai," she said in a silent prayer, "send the hunters far from the rhinos." She knew the warriors must hunt the lion and that they wouldn't hurt the rhinos if they met them by accident, but the sudden appearance of warriors, ready to kill, could chase the mother and baby from the area and she might never see them again. She couldn't bear that thought. As quietly as a leopard stalking its prey, Namelok left her bed to sit outside with her back against the rough dung wall of the hut. Shadow enveloped her as the moon moved behind their hut, and the singing voices soothed her.

She thought she was alone until her father appeared around the side of his third wife's hut. Namelok rose quickly and went to his side. "My Sweetest One, what are you doing up so late?" Reteti asked in surprise. It was clear that his excitement about the lion hunt was subdued, and Namelok was sure she knew why.

"The same as you," she said quickly, "wishing that Loitipitip was here to lead the hunt." It wasn't completely true. Every day she wished for Loitipitip to come, but now she was worried about the rhinos. But she couldn't tell her father that. She studied his face in the moonlight. Three lines creased his forehead like folds in a blanket.

Nodding slowly, he said, "You are right." Then, looking closely at his favorite daughter, he asked her, "How is it that you hear my thoughts even when I don't speak them aloud?" Brushing his fly whisk once through the air, he said, "Go to bed now, for the dawn is closer than you think, and you need to collect wood in the morning for the Naming Ceremony. Promise me you won't wander far, for the lion may be still be near. In fact, take your brother Sambeke with you, for protection."

"That's not necessary," she blurted. "I have a special place far from the water hole where they saw the lion prints." It was such a terrible idea to have her brother accompany her that she added quickly, "Sambeke deserves the right to show the hunting party where the tracks are. After all, he was the one to find them."

A wave of pride crossed her father's face, erasing his forehead wrinkles like a wind smoothing grasses on the savannah plains. "Yes," he said proudly, "he was the one to find the tracks."

Before he could tell her to take another brother, she turned quickly toward her sleeping hut. "Good night, *Papa-ai*. Sleep well."

Looking over her shoulder as she bent to enter

through the low door, she saw her father nod his head, as if in approval. She was sure he was thinking of Sambeke, last son of his first wife. With his head back, and his voice clear, Reteti said to the night sky, "He will make me proud."

Namelok stayed stooped in the doorway, smiling to herself as she said, "Father also has conversations of one—that's where I get it." Still smiling, she watched as he turned and entered Nasieku's hut, and then she entered hers. Sleep overtook the *enkang* for everyone but Namelok, who, no matter how hard she tried, could not get the two rhinos out of her mind. She knew she would see the rhinos tomorrow, regardless of the warriors on the lion hunt.

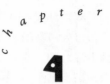
AT THE VERY FIRST glimmer of light, when darkness had not totally surrendered to dawn, Namelok left her bed. It was dark inside the windowless hut, but she knew exactly where the dying fire lay, and skirted around it. Her sister's raspy sleep breath filled the hut. Namelok stretched when she stepped outside into the crisp morning air, laughing when she spotted a small boy sleeping, snuggled up to a lamb. The gathering glow of the rising sun sent red, orange and pink rays knifing skyward. In perfect silhouette on the horizon stood a solitary warrior. He stood on one leg, his other foot resting against the one he stood on, leaning on his spear. Namelok was sure he was awaiting the others to start the lion hunt.

She grabbed a *panga* and strode toward the main gatepost, eager to find the rhinos. She was glad to see that Sambeke was there ahead of her. He lifted the thorn gate out of the outer wall. Loud moos and bleating filled the air as the hungry cattle, goats and sheep responded to the sound. As Sambeke rushed back to release the bellowing animals from their enclosure, Namelok gladly slipped past him, before he could say anything, and waited beside the gate for the hunters to leave.

The scene before her was breathtaking. The acacia stands burst into a yellowish-green shimmer against a sky so blue, she almost reached out to touch it. Not one single cloud scudded across the sky, and the sounds of the day beginning surrounded her. She could hear the low rumbles of men greeting one another, dogs barking, the hunting party gathering, and then the one sound she could not adjust to—a passing truck.

In their previous home they had rarely heard cars. They really only heard them when they were grazing their animals illegally inside the Masai Mara Nature Reserve, on land that used to belong to the Maasai. Reteti tried to avoid encounters, so he told his sons and daughters, "Keep the herds out of the park if possible." It wasn't fear of the law that made him say this; it was his dislike for the tourists with their cameras who stopped to photograph them, with or without their permission. Reteti had seen young warriors on the roadside, actually flagging down Land Rovers to pose for photos. To sell their souls. "Enkai, please spare me the shame of seeing one of my sons ever do such a dishonorable thing," he had said as he turned his head away from the *ilmurani* that sad morning.

Now, in their new *enkang* not far from the road, in fact on the entry road to the park, the sound of traffic was common. Namelok, waiting for the hunters to leave, looked at the four separate compounds, plus the war-riors' *manyatta* standing off at a distance. The *enkang* standing nearest to the road was set up for tourists to walk through. There warriors danced for money and women sold the beaded necklaces and bangles they had made. For Reteti, The Helpful One, it was heartbreaking and disgusting to see.

Namelok would never forget the night her father surprised them all with his unexpected announcement. "Our land is overgrazed," he told his four wives four months before, wrapped in darkness on a moonless night. "The sheep and goats that will eat anything cannot even find a dry sprig to pull out." With a shake of his head and bitterness coating his words, he said, "The land we left fallow last year for grazing this year is now full of wheat. The lowly tillers of the soil, the Poor Ones," he said with a loud suck of his teeth, "have stolen our land, so we must move away this season. Our family will go when the moon returns in three days, so start preparing."

It was Nanana who asked the question that Namelok couldn't get out. "And what about Loitipitip? Shall he leave his age group?"

"No," was all her father said. Then he stood and strode away into the darkness, the sound of his fly whisk slapping against his thigh.

This move had ripped the family apart, Namelok thought, gazing upon the morning colors fading while the sun's light took over. It still saddened her to think of Loitipitip, left behind. He had stood there bravely the morning of their departure as their father told him, "You are a warrior, circumcised and trained together with your age-mates in the skills of battle, cattle raiding and lion hunting." They all knew this, but Namelok watched her father as he spoke seriously. He spun his *oringa* round and round in his left hand, gazing into his son's eyes. "In time you will become Junior Elders together, and eventually Elders that lead our community. Make your mother and me proud," he said, then turned and marched off.

Now Namelok looked around her at their new home—the giant baobab tree across the road that made a perfect gathering spot, and the plains rolling off into the far distance. Her father had found them exactly what he was looking for. When they left Loitipitip behind, they walked for days, never heading to this place as a destination, just looking for the combination of grazing and water—two things not always found together—and companionship, if possible.

Three family *enkangs* had already dotted the landscape when they arrived. Her father had looked around and said, "Perfect. We will stop here if they will have us." Namelok had looked at her mother, who smiled behind her hand. They both knew they would never be turned away, for it was not the Maasai way. A group of Elders had poured out of the second *enkang*, welcoming the family to their place. "We have a deep borehole with plenty of water for all," said one old man. "Your herd looks healthy," added another. "There is suitable grazing not so far away. We hope you will stay."

Reteti had turned then to look at the warriors' *manyatta* and nodded his head in approval. That meant company for his older daughters and protection for his family and livestock. Namelok was proud as he said, "Thank you for the welcome." He turned to his wives, who were already chatting with the women from the place, and laughed. "I guess it's not really up to me—my wives are already settling in." Together his four wives went right to work with their new friends, each starting her own hut while the men and boys cut and gathered thorny branches to build the surrounding walls.

Reteti tried not to jump every time a vehicle chugged by, spewing black smoke and making his eyes and nose burn. But even four months later the sudden hooting of a horn or the screech of brakes sent shudders through his body.

Now the sudden *ka-blam* of a backfiring truck shook Namelok out of her daydream of days past. The warriors were out of sight, so she asked herself, "What are you waiting for? Go find your rhinos." As if someone held a hot coal to her foot, she took off running to escape being spotted and followed. She ran until she reached the far side of the closest stand of trees. With quick glances over her shoulders she looked back to see if anyone was following her, but all eyes were focused in the opposite direction, watching the young warriors running and leaping. The lion hunt had started. Sambeke ran like the wind before them all.

Namelok sprinted across the plains toward the rising sun in the opposite direction of the lion hunters, kicking up her heels like a frolicking Thompson gazelle. She whipped past the first stand of trees, still within sight of the *enkang*. Her necklaces bounced as she sprinted across a stretch of open savannah past a small copse of thorn trees and tall grass. Finally, out of breath and far from the village, she passed a small copse of trees where she hoped to find the rhinos again. She slowed her pace like a cheetah on a failed hunt, winding down to a quiet walk. She knew to arrive huffing and puffing would definitely frighten the mother and baby rhino, so she whispered to herself, "Slow down. Be calm. You don't want to scare them away on your second visit." She froze when she saw them off in the distance. She hoped the wind would catch her scent and announce her arrival.

The powerful noses and ears of both rhinos had already detected her approach. The mother rhino stood as still as a giant boulder, head held high while her nostrils jerked and quivered and her ears stood at attention, one facing forward and the other facing back. Her double horns were pointed at the sky as she sniffed and listened.

Namelok walked slowly, not trying to conceal her footsteps, but also trying not to sound aggressive. Creeping along, she scanned the dense thicket of thorn trees and bushes, looking for a path toward the powerful rhino. Looking left and right, she saw only branches and spiderwebs stretched from one tree to another. She stepped into the thicket, crunching branches as she went, breaking others with her hands. With each snap the rhinos looked more ready to flee or charge, and each time Namelok froze in the tangle of branches. Scratches ran up and down her arms like the reddish trails left by termites along the ground, but she didn't touch them to rub away the pain.

Now, five body's lengths away from them, she took a

deep breath, then whispered in the same voice as the day before, "*Yieyio* Emuny Narok and Siri Aang, *supa!* Hello! It's your friend, My Sweetest One." The rhino's head made the smallest of tilts toward her voice, which gave Namelok an idea. She whispered, "Currrr, currrr," the sound that had relaxed the worried mother the day before. Namelok let out a breath she didn't know she was holding when she heard the mother rhino snort, then go back to her eating.

In her excitement Namelok lunged forward and the mother rhino jumped to her left like a forty-pound gazelle instead of two thousand pounds of muscle, placing herself broadside between Namelok and her baby. The young Maasai girl froze, praying that her sudden movements wouldn't scare the two away. "Sorry, mother," she whispered. Trying to calm the agitated rhino, she used the words of the day before. "Push harder, mother. Push harder."

For minutes neither animal nor human moved. As if in a trance Namelok continued to purr forth, "Currrr, currrr." The mother rhino kicked the hard-packed earth, sending up a cloud of dust. She raised her head higher, drawing large sniffs of air to identify the scent. With another quick snort the mother rhino moved to the side, showing off her baby to the girl. "She knows me," said Namelok, then gasped with joy when she saw the perfect little replica of its mother so close.

"Siri Aang," she whispered in awe, "Our Secret." The baby's ears flopped back and forth, a sloppy copy of its mother's movements. Holding its head high, it sniffed the air. Two little nubs that would one day be horns stuck out of its face, just like the ones on its mother. Namelok had to laugh as Siri Aang tried to look so old and so bold, oblivious to the shriveled birth cord that hung from a body so small, it could walk beneath its mother's belly and not touch her. Siri Aang glanced Namelok's way as the girl called, "Currrr, currrr." Dropping its head, it nudged its mother's side, looking for milk. The mother calmly stood there, feeding her baby and watching the young girl.

Namelok could not stay silent. "She's beautiful, mother!" she said out loud. Namelok thought of the two people in the world she would love to share this with, her father and Loitipitip. When the mother rhino suddenly flinched at the sound of cracking branches, Namelok realized just how impossible sharing this dream with anyone would be. Together they watched a pair of warthogs sniffle their way forward. A small grunt from the rhino made both the warthogs lift their heads, and in no time they were scrambling away, tails raised high as they ran.

The sun was definitely on its way up the sky, so Namelok began to collect wood. The early chill had melted into growing warmth, and the sound of the cicadas grew in volume with each rising degree sent down by the sun. She went about her business, slowly picking up branches and making a bundle to hang off her back, all the while talking to her two rhino friends that stood less than a stone's throw from her. Siri Aang suckled noisily while its mother calmly ripped leaves from a nearby thornbush.

Namelok glanced their way every few seconds, still not believing that they were all there together. With deep emotion she gushed, "I love how comfortable you are with my presence." She smiled, for she knew the enormity of this privilege. "No one would believe this," she told them. "Even my father and brother would have to see this to believe it, but that will never happen."

Standing straighter and throwing back her shoulders, she said with a seriousness she never had used before, "I will do my best to protect you, no matter what that takes. It is my promise to you."

Not wanting to overstay her welcome, or be gone too long from the *enkang*, Namelok finally finished gathering her wood. Bowing her head in respect to the two rhinos, she said, "Thank you for letting me be here. May Enkai protect you, and may we meet again soon." Emuny Narok browsed on with no sign of noticing the Maasai girl, while Our Secret slept at her feet.

With careful movements Namelok placed the pile of wood in her leather harness, then slipped the strap against her forehead while her messy load of short and long sticks hung off her back. She left for home with a bounce in her step under her heavy load.

THE CAMP WAS bustling when she arrived. The Naming Ceremony was only hours away. Her mother held tightly to the bleating sacrificial goat, preparing to slaughter it. Nanana sharpened a knife on a stone, and others were building a fire from the wood Namelok had brought the day before. Her mother waved her over, and the girl dropped her load of firewood and tipped her head in greeting to all the women standing together. One by one they touched her head in welcome.

"You were gone a long time, My Sweetest One," said her mother. With a twinkle in her eye she looked around at her co-wives and friends and continued, "Please don't tell me you were out having a conversation of one. Please tell me you were with a warrior, for that would put my mind at ease." All the women laughed.

Namelok knew it was her mother's sense of humor that made her so popular. In their previous camp her mother had been friends with everyone. She remembered when Nanana told Namunyak, "You are very lucky, for you have a friend in every *enkang* and in every hut inside every *enkang*." Her name meant "The Luckiest One," and she often thanked Enkai, for she said she felt that way.

Namelok smiled shyly as the women laughed, then said, "Sorry, Mother, no warrior, just gathering lots of firewood." They all looked at the pile of wood that rested at her feet beside the already roaring fire. How strange it looked. Normally she broke all the long branches before carrying them back, but today she hadn't because she hadn't wanted to risk scaring the rhinos. She hoped no one noticed. Bending quickly to avoid any conversation, she took a long branch and laid the end in the flames, as if she had brought it back that long on purpose. As the small twigs on the branch burned off, she moved the wood deeper into the fire. It was not long before there was a bed of red-hot coals perfect for cooking the sacrificial goat for the feast after the Naming Ceremony.

Once the meat was roasting, and while the sun was still shining in the hut door, the women crowded into Nasieku's hut for the first step in the ceremony. Nasieku sat with her baby on her lap. She wore a *kikoy* of bright orange, red and gold, and her jewelry brightened the dark interior. Her three-month-old baby was swaddled in a red and white cloth, with a full head of tightly curled black hair that would soon be gone. An old woman silently entered the hut, a sharp razor blade in her hand. Nasieku tipped her head and the grandmother squatted beside her. She said not a word as she started scraping the hair from the mother's head, leaving a glistening pate. With the same sure hands she shaved the baby's head. When she was finished, she announced, "By having your heads shaven side by side, you have entered a new phase of life together."

Namelok sat squeezed in between her sister Lankat and an old woman. Lankat pressed against her right leg, and the crone leaned on Namelok's left thigh. Namelok smiled at them as they waited together. She knew her sister, one year younger than she, was dreaming of the day when she would have a Naming Ceremony for her own babies. How everyone there would laugh, she thought, if they knew she was thinking of a Naming Ceremony too. For a baby rhino.

It was hot and smoky in the hut, filled with co-wives and the many neighbor women who had crowded inside. They watched as the grandmother carefully gathered all the hair, piling it together, then turned to a stool at her side that had a pool of milk resting in the center. Spreading the hair around the milk, the old woman said, "This will seal the bond between mother and child. Tonight, your child will be named." Then, as quietly as she had entered, the stooped old grandmother left the hut.

As all the girls and women filed out of Nasieku's hut, the warriors returned from the lion hunt. But what had happened? Namelok could see from a distance that there was none of the joy of the night before, only a silent line of tall young men, spears in hand, returning. The tallest warrior, leading the line, stopped before a group of Elders, sitting under the shade of the giant baobab tree across the road. He dropped his head and said loud enough for all to hear, "We are back. The lion's tracks were leading away from the watering hole and the *enkangs*, deep into the park, so we have returned. All are safe here, as are all of our cattle, for the lion has left. We, though, are tired, hungry and thirsty. Please allow us to eat, rest and drink."

The quick nods of the Elders' heads signaled they could leave. As they departed, Reteti called out, "Thank you for your quick action. Now go and rest." Namelok watched as they shuffled off. She wondered if the lion would be back—or where it would wander—but now she looked forward to the evening when the warriors would sing again and dance, to entertain the people gathering for the Naming Ceremony.

With the cool of evening Nasieku left the hut, her baby tied snugly onto her back. She went to the animal pen and milked a goat from her herd that strained with her full udders. Then mother and child entered their hut, where her husband and three other Elders waited. Slightly bowing, she greeted them shyly, then sat on the floor with her baby on her lap. The baby squirmed and fussed while the men mumbled, and Reteti stared at the infant. Namelok crouched just outside the short doorway, listening. She wanted to know exactly what to say officially to give Siri Aang her name.

Clearing his throat loudly, Reteti interrupted the three mumbling men. Then, holding his right hand up, he pulled back on his first finger and said to the still-squirming baby, "You were born where you were not conceived." Pulling back on his second finger he said, "You will start life in a place far from home." Grabbing his third finger to hold with the first two, he finished,

"And you will eat things in your youth that I still try to adjust to as a man."

A moment of silence filled the hut, Reteti looking one by one at the Elders and then Nasieku. Placing his large hand on his daughter's head, he announced, "This baby shall be called Nosiligi, which means Born in a Time of Change. Let's wish that she brings with her hope for the changes challenging our life." Then together the four men said to the baby, "May that name dwell in you."

"That's it," Namelok said to herself. "I know just what to say to make Siri Aang forever Our Secret."

As the men left the hut one by one, the women filled the twilight with a joyful song. Happy high-pitched wails cut the evening air as the women sang to welcome the newly named Nosiligi to the family. Kids played loud games of hide-and-seek and lion hunt while the women, old and young, sang and danced, forming a tight circle around Nanana, the first wife, who sang the song of Nosiligi to family and friends.

Nanana threw her head back, showing off her finest clothes and jewelry worn only at ceremonies. Namelok admired her red cloth with horizontal white lines tied over her left shoulder. It draped down across her skirt made of another red cloth, with large white stripes running up and down. Standing in the middle of the circle, Nanana's high, squeaky voice rang out over the harmonious humming of the surrounding girls and women. Namelok stepped into the circle of dancers. They all moved as one, first bending their knees in a small dipping motion, then standing tall, bouncing the layers of beaded necklaces that adorned each dancer. With each bounce Namelok knew that while all the others danced for Nosiligi, she danced for Siri Aang.

Nasieku sat tall at the feet of the singing first wife, her back straight and her legs stuck out in front of her like spears. Holding Nosiligi high above her head, mother and daughter smiled happily at each other. Joy and dust filled the air. The men drank honey beer, and everyone shared the joy of welcoming a new baby to the community and the safe return of the lion hunters. Namelok danced and sang, her heart full for more reasons than she could name.

When the full moon was nearly overhead, and the moon shadows short, Namelok left the group. Stopping to congratulate the tired mother before leaving, she bent low to kiss the forehead of the sleeping baby. "Welcome, little sister. I like your name Nosiligi. It shows what a smart father we have." She was happy for the mother and child, for as the old grandmother had said, "You are now successfully launched on a new stage in life." In some way she couldn't quite identify, Namelok felt as if she were entering a new phase too.

She had no idea how right she was until the next morning, when she was shocked to find blood on her thighs. No one else must know. Especially her mother. She knew her life would change forever.

If she told her mother, the news would be out in no time—she would be delighted that her daughter would soon be a woman. Namelok thought of how her mother asked her every day if there was news, and how she always said, "No." She would go on saying "No." She would lie for as long as she could. "I must hide my bleeding for as long as possible, because it's going to change my life forever."

Shaking her head, she said, "Now I have two secrets, when only two days ago I had none."

THE MORNING OF her first bleeding Namelok realized right away how much her life would change. Sitting with the rhinos during the heat of the afternoon that day, she chattered to them as if she were talking to someone who could answer her.

"Mother Black Rhino, please let me come visit every day, for soon my life is not going to be my own." She shuddered down her long spine, tapping her hands on her thighs. Once her mother knew her bleeding had begun, she would no longer be able to wander freely— not to visit the warriors in their *manyatta* or visit the rhinos in the bush. Then with a shudder that shook her down to her ankles she said, "But worst of all—soon I will be initiated, the *emuratare*, and married off."

Namelok sat quietly for a minute, thinking about all the secrets taking over her life. She knew the most important secret was standing right in front of her, her rhino family.

Shaking her shoulders to give herself confidence, she remembered the other reason she was there. Namelok cleared her throat and then called across the hard-packed earth that separated her from the rhinos, "I almost forgot. I know how to connect us forever. We are going to have a Naming Ceremony right now, just like the one we did for Nosiligi yesterday." The rhinos ignored her as she spoke solemnly to the hot African afternoon. The air was a concert of the drawn-out *tee-jeeoooo, tee-jeeoooo* call of a redwing starling flying overhead, buzzing cicadas and the soft sound of Emuny Narok pulling leaves off a thornbush.

Namelok raised her right hand, then pulled back on her first finger and said to the sleeping baby rhino, "You were born before my eyes." Pulling back on her second finger, she said, "You will always be my family." Grabbing her third finger to hold with the first two, she finished, "And I will never tell anyone about you."

A moment of silence filled the air; even the cicadas were silent, as if waiting for the announcement of the name. Pointing directly at the rhino that looked like a small boulder on the earth, Namelok announced to the bush and Emuny Narok, "This baby shall be called Siri Aang, which means Our Secret." Then she said to the baby rhino, "May that name dwell in you." Four times she said it, once for each Elder who had given Nosiligi her name.

IT TOOK A LOT of creativity to see the rhinos every day, and Namelok was shamed by the little lies she told her mother and father. She didn't bring back wood every time she visited her rhino family, for she often covered her trips by telling her mother, "I am going to the *olduka.*"

It wasn't a total lie, for after her chores and rhino visit were finished, she often wandered over to the little shop in the late afternoon. Sometimes her mother even sent her there, in search of needles or a small pile of onions. The tiny wooden building with a sagging front porch sat on the edge of the road, not far from the park's entrance.

She had never bought anything before arriving at their new home. In fact she had never even seen a permanent building before they arrived, much less a store. All their needs had been met by the herd or by barter in the past. Her father traded cows or calves or leather or jewelry for whatever they needed, like razors or beads. Now they lived with coins and paper money, and with choices of things to buy beyond her wildest dreams.

The *olduka* had everything, most of which she'd never seen before, all inside the small wooden building. Each time she went inside she saw something new. There were cans of tomato paste beside long, white, drip candles. Piles of onions sat next to bundles of dried tobacco. She had never seen shoestrings before. They lay in neat piles on the back shelf next to plastic sandals, beer and matches. Bright, sharp-cutting *pangas* were stacked on the floor. Shiny tin head pans filled most of the walls. Quietly, so the shopkeeper wouldn't throw her out, she nudged the piles of tired, faded red tomatoes, limp greens, dried okra and bananas brought from Narok, the nearest town.

At the far end of the counter there were rolled cigarettes from a package, lying in a line, right next to where the usually surly shopkeeper took the money. Older than her brother but younger than her father, his skin was not quite white, but it was far from black. The man's black hair touched his shirt collar, and his fingers were stained a nasty brown from the cigarettes that burned constantly in his hand or his mouth. Some days he treated his customers with a distant stare, his face closed to conversation. Namelok knew that no one tried to talk to him on those days, for he was clearly thinking of his home far away. On other days, when he had a beer tucked under the counter, he could be very friendly, laughing happily at whatever anyone said. Namelok preferred his surly days, for his friendliness always seemed fake and his eyes watched her a little too closely.

All day he sat behind his large cash register with round buttons and numbers that popped up in a glass box on top. And from high on every wall, the stern eyes of Kenya's president, Mwai Kibaki, stared down upon him and all who entered the shop.

Namelok loved the sound of the silver machine the shopkeeper sat behind, especially the gentle *ting* of a faint bell that rang before the drawer flew open. She also loved the conversations of the people who came in and out, many at the same time every day. Shouts of *"Supa!"* filled the air as neighbors greeted one another with hearty hellos. The *olduka* is where she met Stephen, the Maasai ranger, and Joseph, the schoolteacher. Namelok had heard her friends talk of how handsome the ranger was, but though they had all seen Joseph with his students, no one ever mentioned the teacher. He always looked so formal in his long black pants, covered in dust from the knees down, and a white shirt with a pocket that had a dark blue smudge covering half of it from something that had spilled or leaked.

She was greatly shamed the first time she met the teacher at the *olduka*, for he had helped her count her change. She had just picked up her bag filled with rice when he surprised her from behind by saying softly into her ear, "You are new here." He pointed at the coins in her hand. "I think you are also new to *olduka* ways."

Namelok glared at him, but she also left her hand open to show him the coins she held. Joseph smoothed the thick mustache that hid his top lip before counting out her money. He shook his head in disgust as he turned to the shop owner and said, "I think you want to give her the ten *shillingi* missing from her change."

The shop owner blew a little puff of air between his yellow teeth, then waved his hand dismissively at the teacher, saying, "Mind your own business." He tried to ignore Joseph, but the teacher was determined.

Joseph took the coins from Namelok's hand and slammed them on the counter. "*Mzee*, could it be you're tired or have forgotten how to count?" Slowly Joseph started counting out loud, and everyone in the shop stopped to watch. The shopkeeper, anxious to be done with it all, sucked his teeth as he slid the missing ten *shillingi* coin across the counter, quickly turning to another customer.

Joseph nudged Namelok toward the door, gently pushing her as she stood staring at the shopkeeper. Her mouth hung open until she finally burst out, "He was cheating me!" She slapped her thighs and said, "Does he do that to everyone, and to me every time?"

"Probably," said Joseph. Looking down into her deep brown eyes he said, "But you can change that." He stooped to collect a pile of old black books he had left sitting on the crooked bench attached to the porch wall. She could see his eyes shine brightly as he said, "Come to school. You'll learn to count and add and subtract, to read and to write. I've seen you watching us, so why don't you join us?" Stopping on the porch stairs, he turned back to her and said with a wide smile, "Just think of the money you could save your family." And with that he was gone.

Namelok had stopped to watch the students many times. They were all boys, sitting in crooked lines under the biggest acacia tree that stood between the *enkangs* and the road. A scratched chalkboard leaned against the tree's trunk. Sometimes the students sat quietly drawing things in the dirt with pointed sticks, and other times they recited words a nodding Joseph pointed to on the dull old board.

She hadn't really thought seriously about going to school. Namelok was certain she would be just like her mother, raising baby after baby and taking good care of her family. Anyway, she knew that her parents would refuse such a thing, especially her father.

More than once Namelok's father had laughed about the students sitting in the dust and the heat. Just last night at dinner he had asked her mother as they ate, "I wonder who tends the animals while those boys sit on the ground making useless noises?"

Namelok had laughed with all the others at his description, though she had been curious about the sounds they were making. It had never occurred to her that one day she might sit in the group, as the first girl no less, to read and write and repeat after Joseph. It had never occurred to her until the shopkeeper cheated her.

The next day on her way to the *olduka* she stopped to listen to the boys singing a song about something that made no sense to her. Joseph smiled at the head of the class, waving his arms as if chasing bees from in front of his face. When the song ended, he nodded at Namelok and she nodded back, then hurried on.

For three weeks after that Joseph and Namelok met at the *olduka*, without ever planning to. He had given up asking whether she had asked her parents if she could attend his school, for each time she had replied, "When the time is right, I will know it."

Then one afternoon as she carried a bucket of water past, he called her over to his slanted desk that sat next to the old chalkboard under the tree. All the kids were gone, but he sat there, and she wondered if he had been waiting just for her. "I have something for you," he said. Taking a clean page from his notebook, and a pen from his stained pocket, he wrote something in large blue letters. Namelok watched closely as his pen moved silently across the page. He finished with a flourish by underlining again and again what he had written, then handed it to her. "Your name," he said.

Namelok held the paper in her shaking hands. "It says Namelok?" she asked in almost a whisper.

"Yes," he answered. "If you came to school, you could write your name yourself."

She turned the paper around in her hands, and he righted it, saying in a loud, clear voice as he pointed at each letter, "N-a-m-e-l-o-k."

"My name," she whispered again, then folded the paper carefully and tucked it under the rolls of the *kikoy* she wore at her waist. All at once—and it surprised her most of all—she knew she wanted to go to school. She walked away, patting the treasure stuck against her skin. She had only gone a few steps when she stopped and said aloud, "Now I have three secrets to keep."

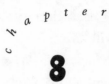

8

IN HER THIRD month of bleeding, as Namelok bent over the twilight fire, her mother suddenly shrieked with joy, "Namelok-ai, your time has come. There is blood on the back of your *kikoy*! Soon you will be a woman!" It was easy for Namelok to look shocked when she saw the stain on the back of her *kikoy*, and so her mother assumed it was her first time.

The look on her daughter's face made Namunyak laugh. "My Sweetest One, why the frown? You should be happy, for soon you will be initiated and marry the man your father chooses."

Namelok bounced her hands on her thighs. "What's the hurry, Mother?" To herself she said, "What can I do to delay what must come?"

She waited for her mother to scold her for having a conversation of one, but no harsh words came. Turning, she saw her mother scrambling out the door, wasting no time in spreading the news—soon her daughter would be a woman! It was what every Maasai mother waited for, and every Maasai girl looked forward to.

"My Sweetest One has started her bleeding," her mother called to Nanana across the compound.

In the darkening light the first wife clapped her

hands and called back, "That is wonderful news." She turned quickly and called to her co-wife Nasieku, "Did you hear the news? Namelok will soon be a woman!"

Nasieku threw her hands in the air and called out, "Wonderful news! When will the *emuratare* take place?"

In the darkness of the smoky hut Namelok covered her face with her hands. She knew that this was anything but wonderful news.

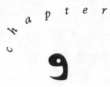

chapter 9

LATE ONE AFTERNOON, as the sun's shadows stretched across the ground, Stephen the park ranger strode over to the *olduka*, anger written across his face. Gone were the silly brown short pants he wore as a ranger, and the heavy boots that must have made his feet hot and itchy. Instead he wore his *shuka*, as red as fresh blood. Beaded bracelets climbed up his arms, and long blue and red strands of beads hung across his chest. A bright red ochre paste covered his bald head, and he held his spear firmly in his right hand.

His eyes flared with anger as he looked first at Namelok as she stepped off the porch of the shop, then one by one at the faces of all the men and women gathered there. His voice carried on the hot afternoon air as loudly as a blaring horn. Anger seemed to snap from his body as he yelled, "If anyone here meets two men looking for rhino, send them my way. Send them to Kakuta the Maasai, and not to Stephen the park ranger." Pumping his spear high, he said, "They are poachers and they deserve to die." A total hush filled the air, followed by a loud chorus of tooth sucking. Every eye and ear was on Kakuta.

Flexing his arm holding the spear over his head, he

called in a voice that carried to all corners near and far, "The first poacher I catch I will spear myself." Everyone there believed him, all nodding their heads in agreement.

A buzz of *Aaa*'s rose from the group of men sitting on the store's porch or squatting down in front of it nearest him. Reteti nodded with the rest of the men until he saw Namelok. Hearing Kakuta's message had stopped her dead in her tracks, and she dropped the small bag of sugar she had just bought, clearly shaken by the news. With a trembling voice she asked Kakuta, "Is it only rhino they want? What will they do with a rhino?" She almost choked as the thought of gentle Siri Aang, growing so quickly and happily, flashed into her mind.

"They will kill it, of course," Kakuta responded. "The rhino horn brings a lot of money, and that is all they think of. And how many rhinos do we have left? Few, I tell you, so we must stop them before they kill one." He looked around at everyone, taking a deep breath to get his anger under control. "It would help if I had many, many ears listening for me. I know they were here yesterday, talking to anyone who would listen, offering to pay money for information about rhinos, so they could, as they falsely claim, 'take their pictures.'"

Throwing his arms up, he shouted, "But they lie. They do not carry cameras like the tourists; they carry AK-47s, guns that shoot bullets faster than the cheetah at full speed." He stamped on the ground, and Namelok flinched. "They came to poach," he said. Driving the pointed tip of his spear's long wooden handle into the dirt at his feet, he shouted, "They came to kill rhino!" His anger radiated out over the Elders and the women and children listening, and wrapped like a tight fist around Namelok's heart.

"They will be sent to you," shouted one old man as he shifted the tattered red blanket on his stooped shoulders.

"You shall deal with them," yelled another man.

Then Reteti's deep, calm voice rang out as he stood and said, "Fortunately, we are Maasai and cannot be tempted. But if they return, we will send them to you, Kakuta the Maasai."

Even though the sun's shadows splayed long across the ground, Namelok took off running toward her beloved rhinos. Her necklaces flapped up and down, and her silver headpiece banged against her forehead.

She fled like an African hare being chased by a jackal until she suddenly heard her father's voice shouting out her name. She knew that to ignore him would be a serious mistake, so she stopped in her tracks. When she turned back toward him, everyone was staring at her. "What sends you running like a gazelle being chased by a cheetah?" he called out to her.

Namelok shivered, for she realized that she had almost given away the secret of her rhino family. A dozen village children stood poised, ready to follow her if she hadn't stopped. Thinking quickly as she ran back to the front of the shop, she dropped her head in embarrassment and told her father and the others who were listening, "Kakuta's words made me feel sick. I was rushing off to be sick alone." Spreading her arms wide and bending forward slightly at the waist, she cried out, "*Papa-ai*, how can anyone kill a rhino?"

Her father's eyes lingered on her, but she didn't know if he was testing her story or considering her question. Finally he said, "Only the lowest kill Enkai's creatures. No one here will help them. Maasai are the protectors of animals. Everyone will send them to Kakuta the Maasai. These men are lower than the Poor Ones, who stole our pasture for wheat fields." He bounced the knobby end of his *oringa* club in his right palm, and then said, "Come, let's go, My Sweetest One. The sun is departing and the cows will be home soon." Silently they walked back to the *enkang*, his hand resting lightly on her shoulder.

That night, Namelok's temper flared again and again as her nerves twisted in her stomach. "Don't bother me," she snapped at Lankat when her sister asked what made her so grouchy. During dinner Namelok shoved her food into her mouth, and her mother reached out and grabbed her arm, asking, "What makes you eat as fast as a vulture fighting over food? Slow down, please."

Namelok tried to calm herself, but the news of the poachers seemed to make all of her problems pile up. The secret of Siri Aang, the secret of wanting to go to school, and the secret of wanting to delay *emuratare* felt like heavy stones tied to her back. There were just too many secrets, especially now with the news of the poachers. Feeling completely out of control, she suddenly announced, "I want to go to school!" Even she was surprised, for she had never said it out loud before.

Her father's eyes shot to her mother's face, then at Namelok. He asked calmly, "Daughter, what has brought this on?"

Instead of answering him she blurted out, "And I don't want the *emuratare* ceremony, *Papa-ai*. I don't want the marriage. Not now. Please, *Papa-ai*?"

Silence filled the hut as all eyes looked her way. "What is this nonsense?" her father asked. "What daughter tells her father what she shall do and not do? Ever since Kakuta's announcement you have been as jumpy as a wildebeest surrounded by hyenas."

Namelok shuddered. This wasn't how she wanted to discuss all these things. Especially not in front of everyone with her nerves jumping like sparks from a fire. She answered in a voice she had never used before with any adult, especially her father. "Why aren't you more worried about the poachers? Why, Father? Why, Mother? How can we sit here so calmly, eating dinner like any other night? How can we? I know Loitipitip would care!"

Her father's eyes widened, and he looked ready to slap his impudent daughter when her mother leaned forward and shouted at Namelok, "Bite your tongue, daughter, for all your words sound like the sputter of the passing trucks. You will not go to school and you will be initiated, sooner rather than later. Now go to your sleeping hut, where you can have a conversation of one that offends no others."

Namelok should have feared the anger in her mother's voice, but her fear for the rhinos left her no self-control.

"Huh," she snorted, "a conversation of one is most welcome." She spun on her heels and stormed off to the sleeping hut, sure that even the goats and sheep wandering in the compound were stopping to stare at her as all the people were.

Jerking about on her hard hide bed, unable to sleep, Namelok thought back to Kakuta's words. That was the first time she had ever heard someone use that word—*poacher*. She had never heard any Maasai even talk about poachers. Why would they, living side by side peacefully with all Enkai's creatures. They only hunted when something threatened them, such as the lion. "Poacher," she said with a shiver to the darkness surrounding her. "Even the word sounds evil. I don't ever want to say it out loud again."

"What did you say?" asked her sister Lankat as she entered the sleeping hut. The sisters were not very close, but at night they often shared stories in the darkness.

With a huff Namelok said, "Go to sleep. I don't want to talk to you or anyone else."

Lankat climbed over her sister, next to the wall, and said, "Huh, sleep. How will that be possible with you muttering to yourself?"

"Just go to sleep," Namelok said again.

At first light the next morning Namelok strode off toward the rhinos to warn them of the poachers. She could feel the eyes of the early risers on her back, but nothing would stop her from visiting the rhinos.

Her father watched her straight back and long stride, wondering where she was going so early and so purposefully. His thoughts were broken when his second wife, Namunyak, spoke at his side. "I see you watching our first daughter, your favorite. Where is she going at such a pace?"

As he shook his head from side to side, his long, empty earlobes swung back and forth. "I don't know."

Namunyak took advantage of the moment, saying, "You must find her a husband soon." Then, pointing at her daughter's distant back, she added, "She wanders off too much. Her head is turned by too many things." Flicking her hand at Namelok's tiny silhouette in the distance, she told her husband, "I would not let her leave now if it was to see a warrior, but I am sure there is no one she is interested in. Let her run, for soon that will all stop."

"You are right," said Reteti. "I will choose someone soon, and stop all her foolish talk." Nodding his head as his daughter disappeared from sight, he said again, "Soon I will choose her husband."

10

HER NECKLACES BOUNCED against her chest as she ran across the hard, cracked earth toward the rhinos' copse. She hung on to her waist with her right hand, to make sure the paper with her name, folded against her skin, didn't fall out. There was more of a wind than usual, coming from the east for a change.

Rushing around a giant termite hill, she came to a screeching halt. There stood Emuny Narok, totally exposed in the early morning light, quite far from where they had always met before. Namelok froze, afraid even to make a sound. The startled mother rhino trotted back and forth like a pacing man, then suddenly turned and headed straight at the young Maasai girl.

Namelok's feet were planted to the ground, as though roots had suddenly sprung forth. Her face contorted in fear as she watched the raging bulk of muscle and anger charging directly at her. Emuny Narok's upper lip was curled back, and she emitted a high-pitched groan. Her head was slung low, and her ears, usually upright to listen for danger, were pinned back against her head. Her tail was raised like that of a mother warthog, and her eyes rolled in her head.

Namelok trembled at the sight of such power charging right at her, and hoped that the rolling eyes meant Emuny Narok could not really see her. She waited until the very last second, then jumped back behind the tall termite hill she had charged around not a moment before. Namelok fell to the ground and worked her way backward on her backside, scrambling like a dung beetle in the path of an anteater.

Emuny Narok skidded to a halt, dust rising high above her head. Siri Aang, who had been running frantically behind, ran right into her mother's heaving side. Emuny Narok snorted and snuffed and kicked the ground, and the dust blew back into her face. Namelok watched the trail of dust and said, "My scent. She needs to smell my scent." With the wind coming from behind her she realized that that was probably why Emuny Narok had charged her—she was upwind of her scent.

With the calmest of motions Namelok rolled to her side and quietly sat up. She hoped the wind was strong enough to carry her smell across the open space to the mother rhino, and blew out little puffs of air with each "Currrr, currrr" that she whispered loudly.

Emuny Narok lifted her head and smelled the air. Her nostrils flared and closed, flared and closed as she took in the scents of dust, fear from her baby, the sharp acrid scent of freshly broken acacia branches scattered on the ground, and finally, their friend, My Sweetest One. With a final snort the huge rhino walked over to the nearest bush and began snapping off leaf-covered twigs.

Siri Aang looked as exhausted and scared as Namelok

felt. She collapsed by her mother, her round belly facing Namelok and stubby legs sticking out. Sucking in her breath with a loud wheeze, Namelok tried to relax. Her knees continued to shake as she straightened her legs out before her. Trying to calm her pounding heart, Namelok took one deep breath, then another. On the third she stopped midway and gasped, "You're a girl! My little sister!" She laughed at herself and said, "I never got such a clear view before."

And that's how they spent the visit— Namelok sitting, silent for a change, Siri Aang resting at her mother's side as she quietly browsed. When the red-billed oxpecker landed on Emuny Narok's back and busily started picking off ticks bloated with blood, Namelok knew that all had returned to normal.

Noticing the stretching shadows on the ground, Namelok realized she had better start back to the *enkang* soon. She was sure that running off like that had not gone unnoticed. Tapping her thighs with rapid little bounces, she announced to the rhinos, "I have bad news for you. Kakuta the Maasai told us all yesterday of poachers that are here." With a shudder and sudden urge to cry she said, "They have come to kill rhino." Staring hard at Emuny Narok, she said louder, "Please, mother rhino, protect your baby and yourself. Run from all but me." The muscle-bound rhino continued to browse, moving away from the pleading girl. Before she broke down in tears, Namelok scooted backward from the peaceful scene, whispering a heartfelt, "Be careful."

When she was out of sight of the rhinos, she stood

and brushed off her red and white *kikoy*. She felt better having warned them, although it had almost cost her her life. A bright smile covered Namelok's face. She was sure she had just passed a test, and couldn't help but say, "Now I am a woman. I have faced the charge of a mad mother rhino, and we both survived." Bending over to collect wood, she suddenly shot upright again and said proudly, "Yes, I am a woman—without *emuratare*."

THREE NIGHTS LATER, Namelok sat beneath a full moon with her father, stringing beads for a cousin's wedding necklace. It was their first time alone since she had been rude to Reteti. She could feel him glance her way more than once. She had apologized the next day, and he had swung his fly whisk her way and walked off toward the giant baobab tree across the road. It was as if a truce had been called, but now she felt compelled to speak. Trying to pretend nothing had passed, Namelok looked up from her beadwork and said, "*Papa-ai*, is it true what *Yieyio* tells me? She says I am to be initiated and married soon."

He flicked his whisk twice, then said, "This is not a discussion. The *emuratare* will be done soon, and then I will undertake a father's most important task—finding a suitable mate for his daughter."

Her looked right into her eyes and said, "Everyone knows that you are special to me, My Sweetest One, and it will take a special Junior Elder to be your husband." He pointed his fly whisk at her and said, "In this moment I see no one worthy of you or with cattle good enough for your bride price. So it won't be immediately, but soon."

She knew he was right. *Emuratare* was inevitable, that she knew for sure. An uninitiated Maasai girl would never be considered a woman. Would never be able to marry a Maasai man, and worst of all, never bear legitimate children. As her grandmother had told her many times, "A woman's greatest joy and contribution to the family wealth is birthing many children." Namelok-ai had every intention of being a mother one day, a proud and good Maasai mother, but not now. Not yet—for more and more reasons.

She had no idea how long the rhinos would remain so easy to find, or how long the mother would tolerate her presence. All she knew for sure was that the *emuratare* was followed by four months of isolation, the first weeks in total seclusion. The rhinos would never remember her after such a long time, if they were even still around by then.

"It is a tradition we will not give up," her father said in the glowing moonlight, bursting into her thoughts. She noticed that his voice had lost its tenderness, taking on an edge.

"Don't worry, *Papa-ai*," she said, dropping her beadwork into her lap. "I want to become a woman, and marry and have babies." She looked right into his eyes. "But not yet, please!"

She wrung her hands and touched the spot where her written name rested against her skin. "I am proud to be Maasai, *Papa-ai*, but not all the old ways are the only ways." Her words surprised even her.

Before she could continue, Reteti retorted, "Huh!

Someone needs to be connected to our traditions. And you, are you ready to call the traditions practiced by your *Yieyio* and *Kokooo* and all the women before them, old?" He sucked his teeth loudly and his building anger filled the night.

Namelok quickly said, "Father, no, never. I am only saying that not all new ideas are bad. Won't you admit that the borehole for water is good? And that the shop that is a ten-minute walk instead of two days is good? And the school?" she decided to throw in.

Tilting his head, eyes closed, he looked as if he were listening to inner voices for guidance, but Namelok knew he was fighting to control his temper. Reteti put his fly whisk at his side, then raised his right hand about shoulder height. "The borehole, fine. It is good for the cattle and the herders, and you girls who carry water."

Then he snapped up his left hand and said, "The *olduka*, who cares? When it is only a cow's breath away, it makes you spend money that's too little on too many things you don't need." After a moment's thought he added, "It is good for some afternoon entertainment, but I would be happier to live far from it."

Then with a suddenness that shocked Namelok, a bulletlike crack filled the air as he clapped his rough hands together. "That is what I think of the school. May it disappear!"

These were very strong words for her father, especially a man called Reteti, named for his reputation as a man who helps all others. Wishing misfortune on others was something she never expected. How unhappy he was in their new home. She touched the paper with her name for strength once again. "I want to go to school, but he hates that place, and I want to delay my *emuratare*, and he hates that idea," she whispered under her breath. "I need to choose which one to fight for." Her father laughed, for he too knew that My Sweetest One was forever talking to herself, much to her mother's shame.

"Are we in a conversation of one or two?" he asked her.

Namelok took a deep breath as she leapt into a place she'd never been before, disagreeing with her father. "I don't think the school is so bad, *Papa-ai*," she said. "The kids who go can read the marks on a page, they can write their numbers, and they can write their names."

Namelok reached into her waist and started to pull out the paper with her name on it when her father pointed his fly whisk at her face. "Please stop." His glare was as penetrating as the tawny eagle that often sat perched at the top of the baobab tree across the road.

With a scowl crossing his face he said, "Please stop right now. Already you are a rude young woman, something I would never have thought possible. We have been here for only the last five risings of the new moon, and already you question me? You disrespect me?"

He shook his head from side to side in wonder. A quick laugh, almost like the coughing call of the leopard, burst from his lips. "You would really turn your back on being a woman to sit under the trees in the dust and the heat, repeating senseless and useless things that sound like goats belching or donkeys braying!" He snorted in disgust, the angry sound floating on the evening's cool air.

Namelok sat silent, lost for words for an answer she didn't have, when a passing man, perhaps one age-set younger than her father's age group, suddenly entered into their conversation. They had never seen him before, but it was clear he had stopped in the night shadows to listen to their conversation, uninvited. He wore a black beret tilted back on his head, and three cloths, black, white and red draped over his shoulders, right-left-right. Two large silver rings adorned each hand. Had he really stopped to listen to their conversation?

Both Reteti and Namelok were shocked by his behavior, for he did not even begin with the traditional greetings, instead blurting out, "Old man, do my eyes and ears play tricks? For your face looks many years younger than your thoughts." He twisted one of his large silver rings in the moonlight and said, "School is the future—the hope for all young Maasai. You talk like a man born into my grandfather's age group."

Namelok-ai watched her father's stature stretch even as he sat on the ground. "And who are you?" Reteti asked the stranger.

"I am a visitor, amazed by what I have just heard."

"Huh! Do you always sneak up on people and listen to private conversations?"

"No," replied the stranger, "but how can I not comment on something so old-fashioned?"

Reteti's voice filled the darkened space between

himself and the rude stranger. Boiling like a smoking volcano, his words came directly from his heart. Looking up at the stranger, he said, "Today I still raise my children traditionally. The boys get circumcised, become warriors, and grow to be men." His voice rose as he said, "My daughters also celebrate the *emuratare*, marry and continue the family line." In a voice Namelok had never heard before, her father shouted, "They DON'T sell their photos to tourists. They DON'T go to school. And they DON'T challenge their father.

"You hear that?" he whispered as he slapped the ground and grabbed his giraffe-tail fly whisk.

Shaking it up at the stranger's face, he said in a voice that shook with a building rage, "I still have my fly whisk, as in the past. I still have my honey beer calabash. I still belong to the *Iseuri* age-set. You hear that?"

In almost a whisper he continued, "As of nowadays, when I see all of these changes, I hate them. The government people want to stop our *ilmurani* from warriorhood days. They want to educate our boys and girls—for what good? They continue to steal our land as they have stolen our cattle. Not just changes, but bad changes. I HATE THEM! I want my freedom to be Maasai back!"

Silence followed his words. Even the calls of the night owl and the constant rumble of the lowing cattle had stopped. Emotion filled the cooling night air, and Namelok-ai sat back against the acacia tree, too stunned to speak. Whispered murmurs filled the surrounding darkness wrapped in moonlight. As usual her father's voice and words had drawn a crowd.

Shifting his *oringa* from hand to hand, the stranger finally said, "Yes, let us be proud of who we are. And thank Enkai that we were youth when boys were still warriors for fifteen years, and only the Elders could tell us when to hunt lion."

Bending over, the stranger swooped up a handful of grainy dust. As the loose dirt ran through his fingers, all three watched, mesmerized, even as it blew away. "But, old man, like sand in the wind, so go the olden days. They are behind us now, and the way forward is through education. Tradition is sentimental, *Kuyiaa*, and out of date. Education is the way forward, Grandfather."

Reteti suddenly stood, rising to his full height to look straight into the stranger's eyes. He pulled the blanket that hung from his shoulders tighter, standing taller as he did. With his voice as solid as the ground he stood upon, he said slowly, enunciating each word in a whisper that sent his spittle flying, "All these changes. I hate them!"

12

EARLY THE NEXT morning, with the sun a giant red orb balancing on the horizon, Namelok stopped to pick up a branch of the soft olive wood to make an *oloirien*. As she stood, she saw the two rhinos stroll past a narrow break through the brush. "Thank you," she called out, for everyone knew that rhinos crossing your path always brought a day of happiness. Already they had brought good luck by showing her where they were instead of her having to search for them.

The rhinos just carried on, mother browsing and Siri Aang standing close to her side. Emuny Narok's lips wrapped around thorns like they were soft blades of grass as she ate her way into a thornbush. Relieved at seeing them safe, Namelok said, "Stay well and watch out for poachers. Trust no one but me."

Emuny Narok snorted and continued to push into the thorny bush as Namelok collected her wood. At midmorning, Namelok strode into the *enkang*, the large stack of firewood hanging from her head strap bouncing against her back. It was unusually quiet, so she looked around. A crowd was gathered in front of Nanana's hut, and they were all staring at Namelok. She yelped with delight when she saw the surprise that awaited her at the *enkang*. Loitipitip! Namelok dropped her wood and said to herself as she ran to Nanana's hut where her oldest half brother sat, "The rhinos were right, it is a happy day!"

Loitipitip rose to hug her, and some of the red ochre on his chest rubbed off on her shoulder. His smile lighted his face as he gazed down upon his favorite sibling. "You have come," she cried out.

"And you have grown," he replied quickly. "Come, let's go find Father."

Overcome with joy, Namelok grabbed her biggest brother's little finger and held on tightly as they headed to the *olduka* in search of Reteti. He had been there more and more as his mood darkened in their new home. Namelok chattered like a cicada, spilling questions forth like a water container with a hole in it. "Why have you come? How long can you stay? Do you miss us? Are you well?" The questions rolled faster than he could answer.

Loitipitip stopped dead in his tracks, turned her to face him and put a hand on each of her shoulders. His beautiful white teeth flashed from the smile that covered his face. "Slow down, slow down," he said. "You are like a dog chasing its own tail! I'll tell you why I am here when we find Father." Tapping her shoulders, he answered her other string of questions. "I'm not sure for how long I am here." Adding another tap, "I miss my family every day, especially you and Father." Adding a squeeze this time, "Oh, and yes, thank you, I am well."

As they walked, Namelok told Loitipitip, "I hope your presence will cheer Father."

Loitipitip squinted as he looked deeply into his sister's eyes. "Father is not well?"

"No, no," she answered, "he's not sick. He's just not happy here. I am afraid I might be part of the problem." Taking a deep breath, she said, "But we can discuss that later."

Just then they heard the shouts from behind. Namelok had forgotten that Reteti was tending an expectant cow and was not at the *olduka* that day. Brother and sister turned as one to watch the group of kids that circled Reteti as he rushed toward them. His red blanket flapped in the wind, and the tin cans in his earlobes sent sparks of light as they bounced in the sun. The boys around him, each jumping high, shouted, "Your son, he's here! He's here!"

The smile that lighted Reteti's face when he saw Loitipitip touched Namelok's heart, making her eyes water, much to her embarrassment. His eyes glowed, his step sped up and his usual reserve disappeared like a puddle in the sun. Reteti's sandals flapped as he rushed toward his eldest son.

Loitipitip ran like a little boy to his father, bending down and dropping his head of braids and ochre, awaiting his father's touch. Reteti placed both hands on his son's red head, emotion filling his face and voice as he said, "My son, the warrior, you have come." Leaving his hands in place, he looked heavenward and said, "Thanks to you, Enkai, for bringing my son. I send you as many thanks as there are cattle on this earth." Loitipitip stood tall as his father released his head, and Reteti tilted his head back slightly to look his son in the eye. "You have grown tall like a young giraffe. I will be proud to introduce you to all the Elders of our new home." His voice caught for a moment, his happiness hard to contain. "Tell me of my age-mates and our old home, and why you have come this great distance."

Loitipitip's smile made it clear that he had only good news for his father. "First, it is as my favorite sister says— I have missed my family greatly." His smile spread across his dark face toward his ears, stretching the two streaks of ochre decorating each cheek as he continued, "And I have come to tell you that the *Eunoto* Ceremony is near." Standing even taller, he said, "As you know, respected Father, I need my mother to help me pass from a warrior to a Junior Elder, for she is the one who must shave my head." Then, dropping his gaze to his sister, he added, "I would be greatly honored if you and My Sweetest One were also there."

Reteti looked at his two favorite children, his eyes softening with a rush of affection he could not hide. "Come," he said, "there is much to do." Clapping his hands at the young boys who stood watching them, he shouted, "Bring me the cow with the star on its forehead. We'll be by the acacia tree with the heifer that shall soon have a baby." Swatting his fly whisk at the boys, he rustled them off. "Go and be quick. There is much to celebrate."

Namelok, Reteti and Loitipitip walked quickly to the

acacia tree where her father had spent the morning. Standing beneath it was a dark brown, almost reddish she-cow. Her bulging sides made Namelok think of her first meeting with Emuny Narok and Siri Aang. Of the day she helped the wild mother rhino give birth. It took all her willpower not to tell her father and brother right then and there about her other family.

As they waited for the boys to arrive with the cow Reteti had sent for, Namelok looked at her brother, Loitipitip, named for a famous Maasai. Namelok knew little of the outside world, but all Maasai children knew of the famous Oloitipitip, born in a drizzle and killed by an assassin. He was the first Maasai in the Kenyan parliament, killed mysteriously. People had high expectations for boys named after Oloitipitip, and Namelok knew that her brother was no exception.

He was in his fourth year of his life as a warrior. He was the first son of her father's first wife, born seventeen years before. Reteti called his first wife Nanana-ai, My Fruitful One. She had produced four sons and five daughters, and of them all, Namelok loved Loitipitip the best. They used to herd together, first going out with the calves that did not stray far from the *enkang*. When they moved up to goats and sheep, they often spent whole days together. She would never forget the joy of chasing after herds of zebra or wildebeest, stirring up dust clouds that would envelop them. Like tumbleweeds in the wind they ran across the plains in hot pursuit of animals they knew they would never catch. And now this same herd boy was a respected *olmurani*.

He was so handsome in his warrior dress. Her eyes, after five months of not seeing him, gazed at his long, slender body and the clumps of thin braids, bright with shiny red ochre, that dropped down his back. A little collection of short braids fell over his eyebrows, clipped with a bright metal clasp that had been made for him by his mother. He wore a red cloth *shuka*, like a toga, draped off his left shoulder, barely reaching a hand's span down his thighs. A beaded choker circled his neck, decorated with a large white button. Looser strings of black and red beads hung down his chest, and a string of blue beads, exchanged between sweethearts, rested on top of all the necklaces. How fine he looks for just everyday life. To see him dressed for a ceremony would really attract the young women, she thought with pride.

Loitipitip glanced at his sister, who was watching him closely. Crooking his head so the sunlight shone off the ochre on his dangling braids, he asked, "Will you attend my *Eunoto* Ceremony?"

Namelok nearly blurted out, "And leave the rhinos? I can't!" She was amazed that that was her very first thought, and happy that she had held it inside.

Instead her father cleared his throat and said, "I am surprised you don't know, eldest son, for talk travels faster here than the dust devils on the land." He looked directly at his daughter and said in a high voice, rich with tenderness and respect, "Namelok-ai has her own ceremony coming up."

A stilted silence followed, and then Loitipitip let loose with a great whoop of joy, "EEEE-I, EEEE-I!" Now they were both staring at her, wide smiles on their faces. Namelok kicked a stone on the ground, too embarrassed at first to look up. Slowly she tilted her head to look at them as she admitted to herself that she liked being the focus of the two men in her family she loved most. Lost for words, she was greatly relieved when they heard the bellowing pregnant she-cow waiting beneath the tree.

Reteti strode over to the cow and petted its back. "We shall celebrate the gift of your arrival and the upcoming *Eunoto* Ceremony." Then, turning to Namelok, he said, "Please go and fetch my bow and arrow, and bring Nanana, for she must hear the news that her warrior son will soon be a Junior Elder. We will drink the cow's blood on this very special day. Go quickly."

Loitipitip's and Namelok's eyes locked at this announcement, for the drinking of blood was a rare and special event, usually done only during ceremonies, or when a woman gave birth, or when someone was ill. This was indeed a special day, and Namelok remembered again how it had begun with the rhinos crossing her path, promising her a day of happiness. She took off running for the *enkang*, her heart full, the happiest she had felt since meeting the rhinos.

The boys soon arrived with the cow Reteti had sent for. She was a beautiful brown and black Zebu with a white star on her rusty brown forehead, with long curving horns and an udder that never ran dry. Reteti ran his hands along her tall back, her skin clean and healthy. His love of the healthy cow was evident as he rubbed the animal's sturdy withers and thick neck. "It is too long since I have drunk the blood of a cow," he told his son. "We shall celebrate with the blood of the best from my herd." Together they watched Nanana and Namelok hurry toward them.

Nanana wasted no time calling out, "What is going on? Why does she have your ceremonial bow and arrow?" She panted from hurrying after Namelok from the *enkang*. "Are we celebrating our son's arrival?"

Reteti took the tools from his daughter. He would do the blood drawing himself. Kneeling close to the cow, he shot the arrow into her neck, right into the large jugular vein. He quickly put a gourd beneath the arc of blood that shot out of the cow's neck, catching the spouting red fountain in it, making certain not to spill a drop. When the gourd was nearly full, he bent to a pile of fresh dung, grabbed a handful and patted it over the puncture wound, stopping the blood flow as quickly as it had begun. The cow walked off, no more bothered than if she had been attacked by a swarm of tsetse flies.

Handing the gourd to his first wife as a sign of respect, he said, "Today brings many memories of the past and expectations of the future. I had thirteen years as a warrior with my age-set. We were known through-out Maasailand as the finest of fighters. In those days cattle raids were a Maasai's right rather than a breaking of someone else's laws." His eyes looked off into the distance as he said, "A *manyatta* was expected to increase the herds through cattle raids, and hunting lion was an honor and a goal. But all those things are changing." The slightest of headshakes punctuated his frustration.

Nanana stood still with the gourd in her hands. Her eyes were planted on her husband's face like a tick stuck on a cow's hide as Reteti continued, "Today our eldest son has announced the coming of his *Eunoto* Ceremony. He wants his mother to attend, and if you are up to the long walk back to our old *enkang*, I encourage you to go, for only once will a young man take such a great step. It is a mother's duty and her honor, and I hope that you will go with me."

Namelok watched silently as her father nodded his head for Nanana to take the first sip of ceremonial blood, which she did. A mustache of deep red formed on her upper lip as she savored the taste. "With this sip," she said, "I welcome our son, and honor you, my husband. And I thank Enkai for this surprise visit that I have wished for every day since we settled here." The first wife took another little sip and couldn't hide the smile that lighted her face. "Of course I will attend the *Eunoto*. It is a mother's dream and a mother's pride," she said as she passed the gourd back to Reteti.

He took it with both hands and said, "There are so many changes in our life. Even our food," he said with the slightest hint of disgust. Looking into the bowl of blood, he said, "As a youth the cows provided us with everything we needed—meat, milk, blood, leather, shoes, even mattresses." He snorted once and said, "Now the food of the farmer is sneaking into our diet, and most days we eat grain raised by some planter and cooked by one of my wives."

Taking a deep breath and raising his voice to the sky,

he lifted the gourd higher and said, "But today we follow the ways of our youth, drinking the blood of a favorite cow, partaking in an old tradition, making ourselves strong for whatever the future holds. I welcome you, son, and look forward to watching you become a man."

He took a very large gulp, his neck undulating as the heavy liquid poured down his throat. Licking a thick layer of blood off his upper lip, he handed the gourd to Loitipitip. The young man bowed his head briefly, then put the gourd to his lips, his loud slurp suddenly covered by a long, low *mooooooo* from the waiting heifer. Her time was at hand.

Reteti took the gourd from his son's hands and passed it to a group of gathering Elders, saying, "Please drink. Today we welcome my eldest son, Loitipitip, soon to be a Junior Elder." Then he nodded at Namelok and said, "And the coming *emuratare* ceremony of my daughter Namelok-ai." Looking at the she-cow, he concluded, "And the newborn of this heifer." With that he squatted beside the cow as she collapsed beneath his namesake, the camp's *Oreteti* tree.

Reteti's attachment and fondness for his cattle was legendary. He rubbed the cow's belly as she lay panting in the shade of the large fig tree. Many had gathered to watch, not just the birth, but also the man's connection to his cow. He clicked to her with a deep purr, not so different from Namelok-ai's call for Siri Aang. His voice calmed the cow quickly.

Before he had finished his first *chok-chok-chok*, her body relaxed, no more flailing legs striking at the air.

One by one the she-cow dropped her legs to the ground with four loud thumps, and then relaxed everywhere but in her eyes. They were wide open, glazed with a dry, shiny light that reached out of the dark brown pools of her pupils. Her breathing pumped like a cheetah after a sprint.

A sudden contraction sent a shuddering through her body and the birth process began. Namelok watched with pride as Reteti coaxed the cow and called softly, "Push, push hard." To ease her delivery, he pulled the calf by its protruding front legs from the mother's body, timing the pull with each contraction. Soon he had a sloppy new calf. It rested on the ground, breathing noisily until Reteti cleaned the mucus from its nose and mouth. As it struggled to stand, Namelok thought, It's just like Siri Aang, in a hurry to be on its feet. Reteti severed the cord that connected it to its mother as the newborn calf collapsed on its wobbly legs. The mother stood, sending out a long, low *mooooooo* to her unsteady baby, still struggling to stand. When it finally staggered to its feet, all could see that a new bull had been added to Reteti's herd.

Many congratulated him on the new addition to the herd, and all gave him a little nod in recognition, some even spitting on the ground as a sign of respect, acknowledging Reteti's love for his cattle.

The *Loibon* holy man, Saidimu, tapped her father's arm with his fly whisk and said, "Watching you with your she-cow makes me proud. You are what the future generations may never be—a true Maasai." Then he looked over at Loitipitip and said, "Enkai has blessed you, for your son will carry on tradition, but beyond his age-set, uh, uh, uh."

The *Loibon* was famous for predicting the future, and was the man all turned to for advice. Wrinkles covered his face, his skin parched and dry. Even on the hottest of days he wore a thick red blanket over his shoulders and carried a long stick that he leaned on as he walked. A rim of white hair ran around the lower half of his head, contrasting strongly with his shiny black skull. His heavy words, especially the "uh, uh, uh" he had mumbled, rumbled in the air.

Namelok watched her father closely, to see if the dark cloud that covered his face in their new home would return at the mention of dying traditions. But it didn't happen, for her father's pride was great and he heard only the old man's compliments and none of his complaint.

The day just got better and better as she worked by her father's and brother's sides. They carried armloads of grass to the tired cow, collected for this time. It was like the lamb soup they carried to a birthing wife.

Namelok felt her necklaces bounce against her shoulders, her old bounce back in her step. Her long dangling earrings swung in the breeze her walk stirred, making her feel free and pretty and fearless. She felt good, and without thinking she asked her father, "*Papa-ai*, did you know that the teacher needs teaching?" She could have bitten her tongue.

Her father stopped in his tracks, his arms tightening

around his bundle of grass. His eyes darkened, but before he could say anything, she said, "Please, Papa, don't get upset. The schoolteacher and I only talked a few times, and the last time he showed me how little he knows. He is not from here—he asked me if it were true that all Maasai are cattle thieves. Imagine such talk in Maasailand."

Her brother stepped forward and said, "I will teach him a lesson that he shall never forget. My age-mates that traveled with me will be happy to help."

Namelok put her hands on her brother's strong chest and said, "No, I have a better lesson."

Turning quickly to her father, who once again had a cloudy face, she said, "Father, please tell us the story of how Enkai gave all the cattle to the Maasai, and I shall tell the teacher. No blood must fall, for the words of truth will hit harder than the strongest *oringa*. You haven't told us a story for longer than I can remember, and I miss it. Please, Father, tell us the story of why we Maasai are the owners of all cattle."

Immediately her father's eyes relighted and his smile returned. Striding toward the mother cow and her young bull, Reteti said, "Make yourselves comfortable, and I'll tell you the story of '*Inkishu*—Enkai's Greatest Gift'—while we watch the she-cow eat."

13

THE LATE-AFTERNOON sun cast shadows long and deep as it dropped behind them. The sting from the sun's power had mellowed, and felt more like a lick than a slap. Her father stretched out, leaning back on his elbows with legs straight, his left hand lightly flicking his fly whisk. His large ear holes, each holding a shiny tin can, swung gently as he rearranged himself for full comfort. Namelok knew he was happy she had asked for the story. He was proud of their history and always pleased to tell an ancient legend about the Maasai.

"Thank you, My Sweetest One, for asking for the story of how God gave all cattle to the Maasai. Are you settled?" he asked. "For you know how I hate to be interrupted." He cleared his throat once, then began, his deep voice wrapping itself around Namelok-ai, as it always did.

"Long, long ago, Maasinta, the father of the Maasai, lived in what is now the northern Rift Valley of Kenya, in the settlement of Kerio. He and his family lived side by side with all the *engwesi*, all the wild animals that lived on the plains, and when the herds left each year during the dry season, Maasinta and his family suffered greatly. While the wild animals migrated to new grazing, Maasinta and his servant Oltorroboni spent all their days hunting for animals for the family's food pot. Like all life, Maasinta grew too old and too tired for such long hunts, so he went to Enkai with a plea. 'Please, Great One, can you give us animals that will stay with us all year and for all time?'"

Namelok smiled as Reteti's voice rose an octave. "A powerful female voice replied, 'Stand at the edge of the great valley at twilight on the tenth day. Then I will give you my answer.'

"To be sure, on the tenth day Maasinta slaughtered a large wild buffalo and dedicated it to Enkai. Not a single morsel of the precious meat passed his lips after it roasted on a large fire. The smoke flowed heavenward, and before long, thunder filled the air, followed by the voice of Enkai. 'You must build a large *enkang*, big enough to house your family and the animals.'

"Maasinta and his family got right to work, building short rounded huts of sticks, mud and bark fiber, surrounded by a tall wall of thorny branches. Enkai looked down and was content, so she said, 'Now cut down some more thornbushes and build a circle in the middle of your *enkang*.'

"When Enkai was satisfied with the circle, she said, 'On the next new moon you shall get your animals. You, my obedient and respectful Maasinta, must remember one thing: Not a word can be spoken until the last animal arrives from heaven.'"

Reteti's voice dropped as he said, "Maasinta made a big mistake, though, for he neglected to tell his servant

Oltorroboni all of Enkai's instructions. On the evening of the new moon Maasinta went to the edge of the valley, to pray and await his gift from heaven." Namelok jumped as her father slapped his hands together and said, "A clap of thunder brought Enkai's full, rich voice. 'You and your future generations are chosen to guard over my special creation. This creation will keep you well fed and always with milk. It will provide clothes and shelter for you and all the families to come. I call my special creation *Inkishu*. Cattle.'"

In a whisper that filled the growing dusk, Reteti said, "Maasinta continued to pray when a whacking crash of thunder and a flash of lightning pierced the darkening sky. Suddenly there appeared a long leather strip from the heavens, and soon it was filled with the constant stream of the most beautiful animals Maasinta had ever seen. They were huge healthy beasts, with widespread horns and shining hides. The females had healthy babies and full udders. The big animals crowded into the circle of thorns. And all from the love of Enkai. Maasinta's prayers were answered."

Looking from Namelok to Loitipitip, Reteti leaned closer. "The beautiful animals continued to run down the great leather strap, but they crowded closer and closer together inside the fenced *enkang*, an excited Oltorroboni, who didn't know all the rules set out by Enkai, called out, 'There are so many!' No sooner had the last word parted his lips than the leather strap vanished, and not another cow descended from heaven.

"An outraged Maasinta turned to Oltorroboni and hurled a curse, sending him out into the wild, never to return. He also swore, 'I will not give a single cow to you, and you can be sure that the milk will always be a poison to you.'

"When Maasinta returned to his *enkang*, all the family was very excited about the beautiful animals, and thanked Enkai for showing them just how much she loved the Maasai."

Reteti took a deep breath before continuing. "But Oltorroboni was miserable, struggling in the forest. He begged Enkai for cattle of his own, but he was refused. Instead, Enkai gave him a bow and an arrow and said, 'Go forth and kill what you need to live by, as you did in days past.'

"For four days he struggled with the weather and the bow and hunger, and then he went back to Enkai to beg once again for cattle. But the powerful one refused, telling Oltorroboni, 'You must make use of the wild animals that I have given you.'"

Reteti suddenly sat up, continuing with his story as he rested his back against the tree behind him. "Oltorroboni made friends in the forest, with a snake and an elephant. One day he suspected the snake of doing him harm, and so with a single swing of his *oringa* he killed it. The elephant was saddened by the death of the snake. Not long after, a great drought came. All the pools dried up except for one, where the elephant and her baby liked to graze, drink and bathe."

Shaking his head, Reteti regretted the words that followed. "One day they muddied the waters when Oltorroboni came for a drink. In a great temper he made an arrow and killed the mother elephant. The young orphaned elephant was angry and decided to move away, to a place of better grazing and plenty of water, and far from Oltorroboni. It was there he met Maasinta and told him his sad story. At once Maasinta told the elephant, 'You have nothing to fear from Oltorroboni, for from now on I shall protect you.'

"And from that day on the Maasai have been the sole owners of all the cattle, and the friends and protectors of all wild animals."

When Reteti finished telling the story, the half-moon hung suspended like a bright orange bowl over his left shoulder. His last words hung in the air until the chatter and teeth sucking began. Namelok looked around her, amazed to see the crowd that had gathered. So absorbed had she been in the story that the arrival of many more old men and boys, young girls and old women had gone unnoticed.

Her father's final words rang through her head. "We are the friends and protectors of all wild animals." At that moment she thought again that she must tell him about Emuny Narok and her baby. She must! But then it would no longer be her secret. With a great sigh of relief she thanked Enkai for her father, whom she loved so much. She knew she didn't have to reveal her secret family—they would be safe surrounded by her people, the Maasai. In the midst of the talk of all who had listened, she said under her breath, "We are the friends and protectors of all wild animals."

It never crossed her mind that one day she would feel betrayed and baffled by those same exact words.

NAMELOK WAS TIRED the next morning, for the night had passed in dance and song as the local warriors showed off for Loitipitip and his *ilmurani*. A deep resonant chorus of voices had chanted "En-haha, En-haha," setting a rhythm for the bouncing, stretching, dipping dance they did as one, without ever moving their feet. Namelok felt pride again as she remembered Loitipitip's dance. He had moved suddenly out in front of the line of bouncing singers, leaping straight up into the air, driven higher and higher by the powerful chanting voices.

With his hair flying over his head with each jump, his feet rose higher and higher off the ground. Six, seven, eight times he leapt upward, until as suddenly as he had started, he stopped, stepping back into the line. Namelok smiled as she remembered glowing with pride, bouncing her necklaces harder and harder with each deep knee bend and flip of her shoulders in the group of girls that danced in a circle around the warriors.

She had gone to bed late, and woke reluctantly at the usual hour for rising. Groaning, she turned on her side as she squinted through her eyelashes at the early-morning light pouring through the smoke hole. Lankat laughed at the sound and asked her sister, "Too much dancing?"

Namelok knew she would never complain about such a thing, for she could never dance too much or too often.

"No, little sister," she replied, "just not enough night for both dancing and sleeping." Because she started the day slowly, her chores took longer than usual. She arrived late in the afternoon to visit the rhinos. She was eager to tell them of her brother's visit, and was disappointed not to find them there, in the copse. The tangles of bush and branches could no longer hide them from her, for her eyes were used to seeing through the maze, so she knew they were not there.

She would find them. The afternoon sun scorched the earth and all who lived upon it. Namelok had arrived at the copse parched. She first went to the spot of the *enkosikos* squash to see if there was one ripe enough to pick, but with no rains there were no new squash.

Every day the sun had felt hotter and the sky was a darker shade of red, covered by a shroud of building dust. Dust, dust, dust. From the cattle and goats walking slowly, and the passing cars. "Even the kids playing tag stir up private dust devils as they dodge one another's touch," she said as she searched the thicket beyond for the rhinos.

The rains were not due for another cycle of the moon. Namelok shaded her eyes as she looked around her, facing first north, then south, east, then west. Only cracked earth and distant dust devils filled her gaze.

Now, more concerned, Namelok scoured the earth for tracks, either human or animal, as she whispered out

loud, "Please, Enkai, keep them far from the poachers."
With great relief she finally found the tracks of the
mother and baby rhino. Dropping to her knees, she said
to the air buzzing with the hum of cicadas, "Emuny
Narok, how did you get this funny footprint?" Tracing it
with her finger, she said, "It looks like an old man missing an ear."

Bouncing her fists on her thighs, she slowly followed
the two sets of tracks, large and small, mother and baby.
She wanted to share Loitipitip's visit with them.
Watching her feet follow the clear tracks in the light
powdery dust, Namelok wandered past stands of tall
dried grass and termite hills built upon a large fallen
tree, out onto a wide savannah plain. Flat-topped acacia
trees stood off in the distance, and a small herd of eland,
giant graceful antelope with spiraling horns, walked
across the dried ground that seemed to waver in the
heat. They walked slowly in the hot afternoon sun,
heads down, tails flicking off the flies that always gathered in the hottest part of the day. They marched slowly
in the same direction of the rhino tracks, and suddenly
Namelok knew where the rhinos were.

"Of course," she said loudly, "you're all going to the
river." It didn't even cross her mind to visit the river to
make sure the rhinos were there. It stood at least another
two hours' walk away, and she knew she didn't want to
make the trip alone.

She had been to the river once before with her
younger brother Sambeke and his herd. She had loved
being there. Hippos rested on the banks like giant red-

dish boulders. The cattle wandered down to the water's edge, sinking in the footprints of wildebeest and antelope, elephants and hippo. It was beautiful, but too far to go to alone.

Looking around at the open plains, dotted with stands of yellow acacia trees and one giant baobab silhouette far off in the distance, Namelok suddenly felt huge and small at the same time. So exposed. She ran back toward the familiar copse of trees that stood behind her, her heart racing from the sprint across the barren land. She ran into a tangle of branches and scrub. Ever since her close encounter with the hyena as a young girl she had realized that no matter how much she loved the wildlife, she was still an easy meal for a lion or any other predator.

"Calm yourself," she said as she tapped her hands on her thighs. Then, to reassure herself that the rhinos had just gone in search of water and a wallow in the mud, she said, "Everything, all Enkai's creatures, must drink. They'll be here tomorrow."

Suddenly she wanted to be surrounded by people and voices. She ran like a creature being pursued, through the stand of acacia trees, jumping over the fallen tree trunk like a fleeing kudu, right past the *enkang* and directly to the *olduka*. She heard the raised voices from afar, and could see a great commotion going on in front of the little shop. A group of angry men in red *shukas* and blankets surrounded two strangers she had never seen before. A fat man missing most of his bottom teeth, and a younger one with a floppy hat falling over his eyes, were being pushed and shoved and shouted at. Jumping into an old black truck that was missing a door, the fat man shouted back, "Call us what you want, but if anyone wants to make some money to buy more cattle, you can find us beyond the baobab tree down the road."

"Go, go!" shouted one old man with an arm withered from a lion attack.

"Someone get Kakuta the Maasai," yelled another Elder, shaking his *oringa* over his head. Two young boys in tattered shorts took off running toward the huts of the rangers. As the dust of the truck rose in the air, the crowd turned back to the *olduka*.

Namelok asked an old woman stooped nearly in half, "Who are those men?"

"Poachers," she replied.

Aaa, Namelok said, nodding her head up and down. She felt a shudder of relief run from her toes to her headband, releasing the tension she didn't know she held. If they were here asking for trackers—not in the bush—then the rhinos were, as she thought, at the river. And safe. Smiling widely, she hooked her arm through the old woman's arm, asking, "Can I help you, *Kokooo?* Would you like to sit in the shade of the *olduka?*" Together they walked slowly over to the shop. The crowd was still agitated as they watched the disappearing dust in the distance, but one by one they settled on and around the slanting porch.

NAMELOK SAT ON the edge of the front porch, there, but not really, with all the others. A load of tourists in a bus striped like a zebra drove by with three women waving through the top of their vehicle. Each hung on to her safari hat in the blowing wind. A dust trail rose behind them that all people could recognize from a great distance.

Namelok was surprised to find herself waving back, and even more surprised by the smile that followed. It was strange to have such a fleeting friendly contact, but really quite nice. That was the kind of contact her father preferred—nothing longer than the time it took for a bus to speed by.

She watched two small boys run behind an angry goat. Each boy had a back leg and was laughing until an old man walked by and smacked the nearest boy on the back of his head. They dropped the goat's legs as if they had caught fire, and scurried off. Lankat joined Namelok on the edge of the porch. Namelok had to admit to herself that her sister was a beautiful young girl. Only a year younger than Namelok, she had a bright red ochre mask covering her face, and more necklaces adorned her throat than Namelok ever wore. Namelok scooted over to make room for her younger sister on the edge of the porch just as someone turned up the volume on the radio in the shop.

All talk stopped as a woman's voice speaking Maa floated out of the radio. She was talking about *emuratare*. Namelok turned around and stood facing the front of the store, holding tightly on to the wooden rails of the porch. Her mouth hung open in amazement as she listened, for here she was, just trying to delay her own *emuratare*, and a woman on the radio challenging it.

Namelok stared at her sister as they listened to the angry voice on the radio. "It is time to stop the practice of *emuratare*, the practice of surgery without anesthesia," blared the voice. Namelok looked around her and saw that everyone was listening. It was as quiet as when the crickets suddenly stop in the bush. The radio voice carried on, "Initiated girls are considered women at only twelve or thirteen years old. They don't go to school. They are married to older men and must stay home having babies and caring for the family."

You could have heard the sound of smoke rising, it was so quiet. No one, man or woman, could believe what they were hearing. "Who is this crazy woman, challenging our ways?" one angry old woman with a bald head that shone in the sunlight finally shouted.

"Have you ever?" said the woman Namelok had helped over to the *olduka* just moments before. "She may speak Maa, but she cannot be one of us with such foolish thoughts."

Then through the din of rising voices came the radio

voice again, and all stopped to listen, too amazed to turn it off. "It starts with *emuratare*, but we don't want any outsiders coming in and telling us to stop it. It must be us, each mother saying, 'Not my daughter!' Then we can bring about the change."

Once again the old woman spoke out, saying, "Who says we need to change anything?" The other women present sucked their teeth and nodded their heads in agreement with the shouting crone.

People were starting to get agitated, like cattle picking up the scent of a lion, as the speech continued. Some had risen to their feet, waving dismissive arms at the radio. "Stop the voice," shouted one young mother, baby on her hip, waving in the direction of the radio. But still it continued.

"*Emuratare* is very much a part of Maasai culture; it will not change in a short amount of time." Before the voice could say another word, an angry listener finally reached over the counter and shut the radio off. The silence was filled with teeth sucking and people mumbling and shaking their heads.

Namelok looked at her sister. Their eyes met and together they walked away.

"Did you hear that?" Namelok asked. "A Maasai woman is on the radio telling us not to be initiated? It is amazing."

Speechless, Lankat nodded her head yes. "Who shall we believe?" Lankat finally asked, looking around at the angry faces of the adults.

"I don't know," Namelok answered with a sigh and a frown. "Maybe the voice on the radio?"

"Are you crazy?" Lankat's voice shook as she whispered loudly to her big sister. "You saw all the fathers and mothers who were listening. Not one agreed with this voice."

"I know," said Namelok. "I know. Will you join me if I talk about it with Mother?"

Lankat shrugged her shoulders, clearly uncertain about what she felt. "Ask me again, but I don't think I will agree to."

"Fine. Think about it. But not for too long. My time is here."

She looked around to see if anyone was watching them talk, and she noticed Nanana looking their way. Namelok waved at her, just like she had waved at the tourists not so long ago. Nanana didn't return the wave, but turned and walked away instead. She must have seen them talking. As Namelok watched her leave, she said to Lankat, "I think some difficult times are ahead. But don't worry; if I speak to Mother it will only be for me unless you want to join in. That is your choice. But no doubt about it, difficult times are coming."

NAMELOK RUSHED THROUGH her chores of sweeping the compound and fetching water the next morning. She needed to find Loitipitip and see if he would give her some advice. She hadn't been to the *ilmurani's manyatta* since the discovery of her bleeding. If her parents thought she was visiting there, they would restrict her totally, like a tethered cow. She knew that it was completely taboo for a girl to visit the young warriors alone once her bleeding had begun.

Namelok stood a fair distance from the northern entrance in the thorn wall of the warriors' *manyatta* and called out, "*Supa!* Hello? Is Loitipitip there?" She wanted all within hearing distance to witness her calling for her brother, so no confusion could follow. Under her breath she whispered, "Please, Enkai, let him be there."

Her prayer was answered when he strolled out of the gate. He was so handsome, she thought again—she thought it every time she saw him. He walked tall, carrying his spear in his right hand. He waved at her with it, a salute as he raised it to the sky.

"Namelok-ai, where have you been? Each time I have visited in search of you, you were out gathering wood or water or visiting the *olduka*. Always so busy." Taking her little finger with his own, he led her away from the *manyatta*. "You look so serious. Do you have a problem? Can I help?"

Namelok nodded her head. Taking a deep breath, she said, "My brother, I need to talk to you."

"Yes, little sister. What is the problem?"

"What do you think about school?" she asked without looking at him.

He barked a quick laugh, then said, "What do I think about a grown man who spends the day scratching things on a board instead of doing something useful? I don't waste time thinking about school at all. Why should I? It has nothing to do with us."

Raising her eyes to meet his, she said, "But I want to go to school."

Loitipitip laughed. "I don't believe it. Now, just as you are becoming a woman? Why would you want such a foolish thing?" Twisting the end of his spear into the dirt at their feet, he demanded, "Why?"

Reaching into her *kikoy* she pulled out her worn, creased paper. She opened it slowly, reverently. She held it up, showing it to Loitipitip. Running her fingers under the letters she explained, "It says Namelok. Why shouldn't I be able to write my own name?"

Her brother looked at the paper in awe and anger. "That ignorant teacher did this for you? The one who asked if all Maasai are cattle thieves? You still talk to him?"

She folded the paper carefully and tucked it back into her waistline. "He says I am smart and curious." Loitipitip stared at her, as though speechless.

Namelok fidgeted. "Our family needs money, Loitipitip. The shopkeeper cheats anyone who cannot add and subtract. If I go to school, I can make sure that never happens again to anyone in our family."

Loitipitip looked off into the distance. She could feel his growing anger. He squinted his eyes, and a little furrow of a worry line passed across his forehead—just like it did on Reteti, Namelok couldn't help but think.

"And what if Father learns about your silly idea, and sends Sambeke or another one of his sons instead of you?"

"But they don't want to go to school," she cried out. "That would not be fair."

Her brother laughed a quick cough of a laugh, another thing just like their father. "Namelok, why do you think fair is even the issue? Think about it. If Father goes against tradition, and believe me, this will be a big leap against tradition, then he will not make it even worse by sending his daughter when he can send a son."

Namelok's shoulders sank. "So you won't help me?" she asked.

Loitipitip's long braids swung around his face as he shook his head back and forth. "Namelok-ai, I don't know if I will help you. You are right, though. Father does need money. To get away from this place, he needs lots of money. But I am afraid that the few *shillingi* you can save at the shop will not make much difference."

Frustrated, Namelok pointed behind him and said, "Look, your age-mates are calling you." Eager to have him gone so he wouldn't see her disappointment, she pushed him gently. "*Ashe*, big brother. Thank you anyway. Now go."

He didn't hesitate. Running toward his age-mates, he shouted back at her, "*Olesere!* Good-bye." Then stopping suddenly, he called to her, "Maybe it is Loitipitip who needs a plan, Namelok. Maybe so."

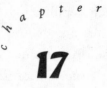
SOMETHING WAS HAPPENING. For days there was a welcome silence about Namelok's *emuratare*, but every day an ever-growing number of girls and women of all ages gathered under the *Oreteti* tree near their *enkang*, to make jewelry, *imasaa* ornaments made only for young brides.

Namelok knew it was an act of love, and an act of community, with each woman knowing that one day her daughter would be the focus of the work. She just prayed the jewelry wasn't for her.

The women sat with their legs extended out straight in front of them, their backs equally straight, chattering and laughing as they strung beads and cut leather. They made as much noise as the weaver birds that flitted about over their heads in the tree. As they worked, the women began singing, always a chorus of soft harmonious voices wrapping around one solo voice. Namelok had often dreamed of the day she could raise her own voice in song, but now she humphed under her breath as she thought that she would be free to sing, but at what cost? Only by giving up all her other freedoms.

She was quietly working on a two-tiered necklace when an old grandmother stopped Namelok's hand as she threaded the beads onto a sisal string. She jumped when the old woman grabbed her hand.

"Namelok-ai, where is your mind today? How can you put orange and yellow side by side? Everyone will laugh at the mix of primary and secondary colors." Taking the work from Namelok's hands, she said, "It is beautiful until this point, so leave the orange and get rid of the yellow. I swear I do not know what you could be thinking."

"I know," said Namelok's mother, Namunyak. "She must be wondering who her father shall choose for her husband." A wave of giggles swept through the group.

Taking a deep breath, Namelok said, "Actually, I was thinking about tradition. Why must one rush into *emuratare*?" She didn't mention the radio program that she had heard only the day before. Nor that the voice had questioned having *emuratare* at all.

Looking up from her work, she saw every head turned her way, and many mouths hanging open in amazement. She had launched the subject that every girl facing *emuratare* discussed with her friends, but never with her elders. Never this way. She had finally opened the door, so she plowed on, running her words together like a cattle stampede. "Why must I hurry? Why can't I go to school and marry later? Must I marry so soon?"

No one answered her, for their amazement was too great. Finally Nanana said, "Namunyak-ai, maybe you are not so lucky after all. Who is this daughter of yours that questions her passage into womanhood as casually as she would ask after the herd?" Then Nanana stopped for a moment and, shaking the earring she was making at Namelok, said, "It's the radio program, isn't it? You heard it and believed it, and now you must forget it. Forget it." She slapped the rectangular leather earring against her lap, then finished with a long sucking sound.

In the heavy silence that followed, Namunyak cleared her throat and said, "Daughter of mine, I am sure I am not hearing the words correctly that fall from your foolish mouth." Smoothing her cow-skin skirt as she stopped to consider her words, she looked at her daughter's face and said, "I have always known that you are a bit different from the others, with your conversations of one, but never did I think you would be so foolish, no, so stupid to think that you can question or worse, delay our traditions."

As an afterthought she added, "Maybe your father has a right to fear the influences here that push young warriors to pose for pictures for the tourists, and now young women to question the stages of womanhood."

"My mother, I would feel like this wherever we lived," Namelok cried.

The first wife looked around at the other girls listening intently to the conversation. Looking over at her co-wife Namunyak, she said, "You said *young women*, but maybe she," she stopped and pointed directly at Namelok, "is only one." Turning back to the other girls gathered, she asked, "And are there more here who challenge the traditions practiced by their mothers, grandmothers and great-grandmothers, further back than we can remember?"

The silence was deafening. Lankat looked at the ground, avoiding her sister's eyes.

Namelok said into the silence, "I do not question all of it, for a woman must make a move from one stage to the next. Maybe there are other ways besides *emuratare*."

"Oh, is that all?" said Nanana. She stood up suddenly, squinting her eyes and shaking a finger at Namelok. "And what would you have us do? Cut your toenails instead and shave your head and call you a woman?"

Namelok's mother shrugged. "What do you think?" she asked the group. "How can we make girls women without *emuratare*?"

Again no one answered, and an uneasy silence surrounded the women. In the distance goats bleated and calves bellowed, children laughed as they chased one another, and the constant hum of crickets filled the air. Everything was so normal in the distance, yet so tense around the women.

Namelok dropped her head and said, "I am sorry, *Yieyio-ai*, for bringing this shame upon you. I will not question it again." She looked around at the other girls and Lankat, who had failed to support her, and then at the older women. "I say sorry to you all. I only wondered if there are other ways to become a woman."

Lankat's eyes still stared at the ground, clearly ashamed for leaving her sister to face the sighs of disgust and anger all alone. The silence stretched like a puddle of water growing larger. Silently, but with as much dignity as she could muster, Namelok gathered her beads and leather and pile of sisal twine, stood, and left.

As she walked away, she kept her back straight and her head high, for she felt proud that she had voiced the things that had filled her mind since the radio program.

They may hate me right now, she thought, but they will respect me one day soon when not even a peep passes from my foolish mouth during the *emuratare*, or during each birth of all the children I will have. She turned back to the group that was watching her. "I will go collect firewood," she said, then gave a little wave.

Lankat jumped up. "Would you like me to come?" she called out to her, but Namelok knew she was on her way to the rhinos, so she called back, "No, thank you."

Her mother also rose. Standing with her hands on her hips, Namunyak shouted to her departing daughter's back, "Go collect your firewood, for soon these trips will stop. Soon you will become a woman." With that the chatter started once again, but all who were there knew it was a conversation none of them would forget.

18

LONG BEFORE SHE reached the copse where her rhino family lived, Namelok began with the soft "currrr, currrr" call. She needed desperately to see them, for she knew now that her time was really limited until her initiation. In the pit of her stomach she knew that her comments had hastened the inevitable, rather than delayed it. "You are a fool," she said to herself. She was so disgusted, she didn't even feel like having a conversation of one.

"Currrr, currrr," she called louder. There was no sign of the animals again. She whirled around in every direction, scanning the horizon, but they were nowhere to be seen. "Calm down. Look for prints." Bent in half, she scoured the dusty ground for their footprints. Her eyes covered the hard-packed earth, so in need of rain. With a fierce concentration she willed the ground to give her a sign that the rhinos were all right.

"Oh, yes," she sang out when she finally saw fresh tracks. It was still easy to tell *Yieyio* Emuny Narok's from all other prints, which showed her they had calmly walked on a path to the river again. She thought of them wallowing in the soft, cool mud.

Greatly relieved, Namelok bent to the task of gathering wood. Her relief didn't last long, for she suddenly remembered what had brought her there so late in the day. She worked with a furious focus, trying to block out the giant mistake she had just made under the tree with her mother and all the others.

Finally she stopped and said, "I am sure I am no one's My Sweetest One today." Grabbing a long branch to break, Namelok snapped it in half with a loud crack. She winced as she asked the buzzing bush, "What if Father hears what I have done?" She shuddered to think of how angry he would be. Placing her hand on her heart, she said, "Not to worry, Mother and Father. I will do as I am ordered. I have no choice."

She straightened her shoulders and tapped the place where her name rested, then placed her hand once again over her heart and said, "But my daughters will have a choice." That said, she felt slightly better. This meant she could concentrate on what was important, making as much time as possible to spend with the rhinos.

Piling the wood into the leather sling, then slipping the carrying strap across her forehead, Namelok suddenly became aware of the quiet. She stopped to look around again. A lone topi, standing on a tall termite hill, looked directly into the sun, facing downwind. The sunlight shone on its red glossy back and shimmered off of the purple swathes on its upper front legs. One horn was broken off. All its attention was focused on something that Namelok couldn't see. She hoped it was Emuny Narok and Siri Aang, but feared it could be a lion, for now that she really looked around, she also saw a herd of zebra, all facing the same way and watching.

Hitching her sling into a more comfortable position, she started walking. A troop of Vervet monkeys sat in a tree, and as she passed under it, they too were staring off into the distance. With both hands holding on to the pile of branches on her back, Namelok nearly trotted back toward the camp. Whatever was out there was something she was sure she didn't want to encounter, or have the rhinos meet either. Whatever it was had gotten the attention of a lot of animals, always a sign of danger. She had enough problems already without running into a lion or a leopard.

It was very subdued in the *enkang*, and Namelok could be sure she was the cause.

The faint *ding-a-ling-ling*, *ding-a-ling-ling* of cowbells floated softly on the air. The herds sent up huge dust clouds in the distance on their way home. Namelok watched her mother as she dropped a piece of wood into the cooking fire with much more force than necessary. A shower of red sparks shot upward as Namunyak turned at the sound of her daughter's approach.

Namelok dropped the wood by the fire, then bowed her head to her mother. It was the first time in her life she wondered if her mother would touch it. There seemed to be the slightest hesitation on her mother's part; then she patted the back of her daughter's head in exasperation. "So you came back," Namunyak said, only half joking.

"Is that all right with you, Mother? Should I not come back one day?"

Her mother pushed Namelok's shoulder and said, "Please, daughter of mine, do not be that foolish. This is the last time we will discuss that which happened today and that which will happen." Squaring her shoulders, her mother told her in a voice that meant no reply was necessary, "You will be initiated in six weeks' time. I still do not believe what I heard today, so you will apologize again to each and every woman, one by one."

Namelok tried to say something, but her mother held her right hand up and shook it back and forth, cutting her off. "If you just do as you are told, nothing will be said to your father about this afternoon under the tree. I do not like even to think about how furious he would be, and the beating you would get. So it is up to you."

Namelok felt a great wave of relief to know that her father would not be told.

"Go find your father now, and we will see how quiet the others have been. I saw him going to the *olduka* some time ago. Look there. Tell him I need to speak with him."

Namelok left by the southern gate. Faint teeth-sucking sounds followed her from the women pounding dinner grain under the acacia tree, where only hours ago they had all been beading. She would begin the apologies when she returned with her father. As she walked, she asked herself, "What will happen to me if he knows? I hope he had a good day."

He had been spending a lot more time around the

olduka, which was very strange. It wasn't as if he were talking or arguing with others, but more as if he were watching and listening, like a cheetah and her prey. It was hard to understand why he did something that upset him so, for anger usually covered his face after a visit there.

As she walked along, a group of three old women from the farthest *enkang* passed her. She greeted each with a head bow, repeating her greeting loudly three times, *Supa, Kokooo*. They waved to her over the distance between them and kept walking. There was no indication of ill will, which made Namelok relax a bit.

She saw her father, sitting on the end of a bench nailed to a wall of the porch on the *olduka*. He sat where he did on every visit, for the space was always cleared for him when he arrived. A glare now covered his face. He tugged on the short gray hairs sprouting from his chin as he listened to two young *ilmurani* argue over money they had made selling their photos. Standing toe to toe and nose to nose, the two handsome warriors shouted.

"I get more because I stopped the car!" said one as he held the money behind his back.

"I get more because it was my photo they took again and again," said the taller one. He shifted his beaded belt over his *shuka* and ran his hand over his long red braids glistening with ochre. Puffing out his chest like a bustard bird, he reached around and grabbed the *shillingi* from the other warrior. This led to a push and a shove, with the shorter warrior flying off the porch and onto his backside in front of everyone there. Gasps filled the air as he reached for the sword in the scabbard at his side.

Namelok froze like all the others till her father's voice rang out. "STOP!"

The look of disgust on his face and the rage in his voice silenced the arguing *ilmurani*. Namelok wasted no time calling out, "*Papa-ai, supa! Yieyio* would like to see you. Can you come?" She was standing directly in front of him by the time she finished her question.

He quickly looked down at his daughter. "Namelok-ai, it is good you have come, for you have rescued me from the saddest sight I have ever seen. Two age-set members, who are supposed to be closer than brothers, embarrassing their whole *manyatta*, squabbling in public like two vultures fighting over a kill, about money earned in a most disgusting way." He stopped and stared at each one individually, saying loudly and clearly for all to hear, "It's best I leave before I say more."

He looked around him and swept his fly whisk to encompass all who watched. "It's best I not come back to this porch, for anger fills my heart every time." With an angry shake of his *oringa* he said, "But today is the worst. Today is the most sickening."

By this time every ear in the place was tuned to Reteti, every eye watching anxiously to see what would happen. Namelok said, "Come, *Papa-ai*, let us go." She wanted to get him away quickly, certain that if anyone there knew of her strange behavior with the women under the tree, they would speak out. The two shamed warriors dropped their heads, and each took a short step backward, the tension thinning immediately. Reteti stared at both of them over his shoulder as he left.

Glancing up at him, Namelok asked, "Father, why do you spend so much time there if it only disturbs you?"

He flicked his fly whisk and said, "Who knows? What else is there to do?" Shaking his head, he said, "But you are right—why do I go there? I am always so aggravated when I leave."

They walked in silence for a few moments. Namelok was greatly relieved. Her father was so calm. He had not heard anything about her. He could not have. As they walked along, he talked, almost to himself, it seemed. Namelok thought of a conversation of one as she listened to his voice.

"Two warriors fighting over a pile of *shillingi*. Disgusting."

As he spoke, two men from the *olduka* caught up to them. Both were Elders from a neighboring *enkang*, perhaps ninety minutes' walk away, who had been among the listeners at the *olduka*. "*Entasupa! Irara kasidan?*" the oldest asked Reteti.

"*Aaa*," her father replied. "Yes, I am well. How are the children?"

"*Aaa*," came the reply, "the children are well."

Reteti then asked, "*Kasidan inkishu?* Are your cattle well?"

"*Aaa*."

Dipping his head, Reteti finished the greeting. "You are all well?"

"*Aaa*," said the old man who had started the conversation. There was a sadness in his voice that did not escape Reteti's or Namelok's ears. "Maybe not all so well. We heard your words at the *olduka*," he sighed. "We are like you, disgusted by what we see." The old man banged his *oringa* against his leg, his agitation growing with each strike. "The young do not laugh at us, but they do not take us seriously either. We must have a Council of Elders and decide what we can do, and act as one. We must stop the selling of photos. We must stop the growing disrespect for us. For our Maasai ways."

The other Elder stepped forward, pumping his walking stick over his head in the air. His voice rattled as he said, "The young people may not agree with us, but they do have to respect us and our decisions." Spreading his arms wide, he said, "All the Elders who live within walking distance should gather and make some new rules. Or better yet, make fines that will stop this disgusting behavior." He shook his head sadly and said, "Yes, we'll make fines of cattle, against the disgusting sight we all just saw. None will want to give up a cow to sell his photo."

Reteti was delighted with the idea. "You tell me when and I shall attend. This council is long overdue." He swung his *oringa* across the horizon and his voice grew in volume. "I shall tell all the Elders I see. We really must do something now. Something serious to save the traditions and culture."

The oldest man pointed to the sky where the sun would be, palm down to indicate the evening, and said, "Tomorrow, this time. We lie in that direction."

Namelok watched her father's face in the fading sunlight. His eyes sparkled. As if his muscles had suddenly let go, his shoulders dropped ever so slightly. He looked much more relaxed than before. Nodding his head, Reteti said, "Just to talk will help. If we say nothing or snap snidely alone, no one will be heard. But one strong voice of all the Elders cannot be ignored."

As soon as they reached the *enkang*, Namelok's mother ushered Reteti into the short oval hut. With just one look over her shoulder her face told all the women and children watching, "Do not disturb!"

It was a strange night. No one talked at dinner, or while they cleaned up. Namelok's father looked at her again and again, but never said a word. Everyone went to bed early, as if all of them were ready for a troublesome day to be over.

The next morning began like any other. The boys wandered out from their huts, yawning and scratching and rubbing their eyes. Indigo rays of sunlight streaked across the sky. Dust from the animal circle hung suspended in the cool morning air. At the first sign of human life the cows began to moo and the young bulls let loose with sporadic bellows. The sun had not yet reached over the thorn walls, and there was a briskness to the morning. The smells of dung and urine filled the air, both odors that went unnoticed, they were so familiar.

Each herd boy whistled a special note to his favorite cow. Some were low pitched and others were high, each full of love. One young boy called out, "*Supa! Inkishu,* providers of all we need. Soon we will walk to water and you will be happy."

Reteti walked purposefully behind all the huts to the southern gate. Nanana called out to him, but he merely held his fly whisk high over his head and called back, "I am going to prepare for the Council of Elders. Please do not disturb me, and do not expect me tonight."

Namelok watched all her relatives, acting just like the topi on the termite hill and the zebra and monkeys the afternoon before, all facing one direction. She followed their gaze and saw her father striding away from the *enkang* and the *olduka*, past the warriors' *manyatta*, in the direction the old man had pointed for the Council of Elders. She didn't know if he was unaware that all were watching him, or just didn't care about the eyes following his departure.

He set out across the wide plain, his *oringa* and fly whisk at his sides and his snuffbox bouncing against his chest. As Namelok watched his proud figure shrink with distance, her mother came up behind her. She wore a purple cloth over her long leather skirt, tying it around her neck as she watched her husband's back like every-one else. She pointed with her chin at Reteti. "He is a man with many problems."

Namelok remained silent. Like her father she just wanted to be alone, so she returned to her hut to fetch her firewood sling and *panga*. Namelok slipped through the southern gate in the *enkang*. She searched the hori-zon for her father's silhouette, but he was gone from sight. There were too many watching eyes to head for the rhinos, so instead she followed her father's path. She walked as if she knew where she was going, but she really had no idea. The sun was getting hot for so early in the morning, so Namelok slipped behind a tall termite hill and sat in its shade.

"I'll rest here awhile," she said to herself. "Then when all are at work, I'll head to the rhinos." As she rested, thinking again about her outburst yesterday with all the women, loud cries of "Yeeeee-ip, yeeeee-ip" caught her attention. Not too far to the east trotted three *ilmurani*, yelping and laughing as they went. She could see that the one in front was Loitipitip, by far the tallest and strongest of the three. He was wearing his ostrich-plume headpiece, the one he had worn into the *enkang* all those weeks ago. His body glistened with red ochre mixed with fat, and his *shuka* was pulled up to show off his long muscular legs.

Namelok looked on with pride, wondering where they could be going in such a hurry. And dressed in this way. At first she started to raise her hand to signal her presence, but she stopped suddenly. Off on the horizon rose a plume of dust, feathering upward and turning the sky a dirty reddish hue. It could be the dust trail of only one thing, for it was compact in size and moving at a great speed.

Namelok slumped against the termite hill, shocked by what she was seeing. The dust from the Land Rover tapered off, then headed across the plains toward the warriors. Namelok shook her head back and forth, her necklaces bouncing as she cried out, "No. No! Please not that!" as she watched the car full of tourists rush toward her brother and his friends. She knew the scene unfolding was what her father had prayed never to witness— all happening before her eyes.

The warriors stopped first, slowing down to a sedate walk, preparing themselves for the encounter. They were close enough for her to hear their voices as they drifted across the wide-open plain. The driver greeted the young men, and soon a discussion ensued. She shuddered as she thought she heard numbers fly back and forth and knew in her heart with despair that they were bargaining for a price. She looked frantically around the horizon, hoping her father was far from the scene. She didn't see him anywhere, just the warriors and vehicle, a giant *Oreteti* tree in the distance and a herd of grazing zebra.

The three young men stood straight as the tourists' heads popped up through the open roof, their black cameras snapping away. One man talked to the guide, who turned to Loitipitip. It was more than she could bear as the warriors began to jump high into the sky, dancing for the tourists, selling their souls for a few Kenyan *shillingi*.

Namelok slunk down even farther against the rough termite mound. She wanted to cry from the pain of witnessing what her father would regard as the ultimate betrayal. It took her breath away. Namelok didn't know what to do, except pray, "Please, Enkai, let Father be far, far away from this terrible sight."

When the *ilmurani* were paid, she hid behind the termite hill, watching them leave. Her heart ached for her brother's shameful act, and she was sure that if her father had witnessed it, life at home would get worse.

19

No one was surprised when Reteti didn't return that evening; in fact they were glad. Nanana called her co-wives together along with all the children and said, "When our father comes back tomorrow or the next day, we shall all welcome him at the northern gate, with loud whoops of joy at his return." Then she looked directly at Namelok and said, "And we will all respect the news he brings us from this Council of Elders, whatever it might be. Do you all understand?"

"I understand. I love and respect my father," Namelok said.

"Then show him when he returns."

When Reteti did not return to the family *enkang* the second night, Namunyak told her daughter, "If you want to attend Loitipitip's *Eunoto* Ceremony, we need to move your *emuratare* date forward, so you will be able to make the long walk back to our old home after the rains." She pointed to the three-quarter moon, painted a burnished red from all the day's dust, sitting just above the giant spread of the baobab tree across the road. "It will happen the next time we see this same moon."

There was nothing for Namelok to say but "Fine,

Yieyio-ai. Let's get it over with. But I don't care if I don't go to the *Eunoto* Ceremony."

Her mother cocked her head to the side, clearly shocked by her daughter's announcement. "You don't want to go to see your favorite brother's ceremony? You must be sick." Her mother had watched her like a hawk the day before, asking her again and again if she was sick, so listless was she when she returned to the camp with no firewood.

"No, Mother, not sick, just very tired." Then to herself as she walked toward her sleeping hut, she said, "The rhinos must be there tomorrow." Looking back at the moon again, she said, "I will tell them I have only four more weeks of freedom."

Early the next morning Namelok rose from her bed, hoping to sneak away, but her mother was also already up. "Are you better?" her mother asked her. She looked at her daughter closely, still stunned by what she had said the night before.

"I'm fine, Mother," she replied. With an ease that scared her, she lied and said, "I slept well; that's why I am up early." She spent the morning sweeping the compound and fetching water. When the sun was at its highest and hottest point, she finally managed to slip away as everyone else rested in the shade of the acacia tree.

She didn't care if they watched her leave. She ran toward the familiar copse. She knew that if the rhinos weren't there today, she would do the unthinkable— walk alone and unarmed across the plains to the river.

Seeing the rhinos lying in the cooling mud would put her mind to rest, she knew, even if they couldn't have time alone together like in their copse. They had to be there, she thought as she picked up her pace.

Once out of sight of the *enkang* Namelok stopped to catch her breath. The white sky hugged the searing heat that danced on the horizon. A somber silence filled the bush, leaving only the sound of her heartbeat banging in her chest. Knowing that she was running out of time was only part of her problem. She needed to know that they were safe. As she raced past a fallen log covered in termite hills, she pleaded, "Please, Enkai, let Emuny Narok and Siri Aang be there, waiting for me. I really need their company today. I really need to know that they are well."

She also needed every possible minute with them. She sucked in her bottom lip at the thought of the changes coming in her life. Stopping suddenly, she held her hands over her eyes to cut the glare, searching the horizon.

That's when she saw the vultures.

They were jumping up off the ground, their huge wings flapping and their gnarly clawed feet fighting midair. One ran wildly after all the others, chasing about like a frenzied mother trying to save a child. Four birds flew off, apparently full and fed up with the greedy one. They fell into the vulture routine of circling high up, riding thermals when possible and flapping slowly when it wasn't. She knew there must be a kill on the ground, for that was the only reason vultures gathered to lurk and fight.

Without thinking about what other scavengers might be there, such as hyenas or jackals or wild African dogs, Namelok charged straight at the spot. She hadn't run so long or so fast since she and Loitipitip had chased the zebras and wildebeest as herders. She waved her arms and screamed and ran harder. Tears were flowing down her face, for without seeing what lay ahead she already knew.

Nothing could have prepared her for the sight. It was the carcass of a rhino, the head butchered where someone had hacked out the horns. All that remained were scattered bits of thick skin, the bones and the damaged skull. A lower leg and hoof, bitten clean away from the rest, sat alone to the right. The hoof was turned her way and confirmed her worst fear. Only *Yieyio* Emuny Narok had the broken hoof that looked like a man missing an ear. Then like a punch Namelok realized that something else was missing—there was no trace of Siri Aang.

Namelok fell to her knees and retched and retched until only thin green bile dribbled from her lips. She raised her head and screamed like a howling hyena. She beat the ground until her fists bled. She got sick.

And then she got mad.

20

"CONCENTRATE," SHE SAID aloud. "Look around, look for tracks." Not far from the scene that she couldn't look at again were the tracks of a lion. It had feasted well, and she could see the impression it left where it must have slept between eating sessions. It may not have killed the rhino, but it definitely had eaten part of it. Her anger about Emuny Narok was so consuming that it didn't even occur to Namelok to worry about the lion and her own safety.

Just to the left of the lion spoor, though, was something else. Human footprints. Showing that three different people had been there. One wore a heavy shoe with circles in the heel. The second had some type of ripples in it. The third was flat, and vaguely familiar. There was only one reason human footprints would be here. Poaching.

The rage that engulfed Namelok drove her on. Without stopping to think about where she was going or what she was doing, she followed the tracks. Her breath pumped forth in angry little bursts, and all she could think of was catching the wretched men that had killed Emuny Narok. With her head down, she followed the prints. She noticed that the circles and the ripples walked side by side, whereas the flats walked behind.

Like a dog on a scent, she followed the prints. Her back ached and her fists hurt, and still she followed the prints, past a tall termite hill and into a small clump of thorn trees. Looking back from time to time, she could see the disgusting vultures fighting over the remains. Soon they disappeared from sight as she followed the three sets of footprints, behind the thorn trees and across a stretch of open space of loose dirt and stones.

When the prints stopped suddenly, she saw the tire tracks. Her eyes traced their path on the ground as she followed them, bent double for a closer look. They made a wide turn, crunching over broken branches and dried, brittle savannah grass. She ran to the far end of the turn-around track for the truck and squatted down. There, lying across the top of the track, a print within a print, were more flat footprints. Whoever he was, he had walked across the track, after the truck had left. "They didn't all leave together," she said aloud. It felt good to hear her voice in the buzz of the cicadas. "I will follow you—track you," she told the footprints. "I hate you," she shouted at the trail of flat footprints on the ground.

With an obsession that gripped her as nothing ever had before, she followed the tracks until they headed toward a bushy area, where Namelok stopped before entering. She stood up and stretched her back and looked around her. The surrounding plains rolled away to the western horizon, where the sun dipped. A vast herd of zebra grazed in the distance, their black and white stripes perfect camouflage as they shimmered in the waning sunlight.

The sloped silhouettes of three hyenas, a creepy sight late in the day, made her take a look at the sun. Her shadow fell behind her so she knew she was walking west, which had to be away from the family *enkang*. She had not only gone a great distance, but she also had no idea which way was home. It suddenly occurred to her that she was going to spend her first night alone in the bush. Not even a warrior with a spear would want to do such a thing. Not even Loitipitip. But she could not lose the trail.

Standing straight and looking around her at the golden glow turning a soft red, she said to herself with a shiver, "Where did the day go? There was not enough of it. Soon the night will fill the sky." Then an even more important question popped into her head and she asked the darkening day, "What do I need to do?" She looked into the bushy thicket in front of her, where acacia trees and thornbushes grew in tight pockets of vegetation. Two game trails crisscrossed through the copse, one wide enough to allow an elephant to pass, the other narrow and hard packed with many cloven hoof tracks.

Namelok knew that buffalo, one of the most dangerous animals in the bush, could be surprised in dense growth. The charge of the buffalo was fast and powerful. *Ilmurani* all dreamt of two things: wearing their own lion's-mane headdress and carrying their own buffalo-hide shield painted the colors of Maasai, black, red and white. Killing a buffalo could earn a shield; they were that fierce and respected. She knew better than to enter the copse so close to dusk. If she surprised a buffalo, she certainly could die. If it got dark while she was inside the copse, she would have to spend the night inside, sharing the trail with any animal that might wander down it. It would be easy to stumble into the thick walls of treacherous thorns. That she didn't want to do.

She stooped down for a closer look at the footprints she had followed. They veered off around the outer border of the copse, and suddenly she noticed spots of what looked like dried blood in the left track. The pattern of the flat tracks had changed, and Namelok dropped to one knee. Slowly she traced her finger around a short little skid mark of a print, and then drew an arrow back to the little puddle of blood. Then she traced around the complete flat foot.

Scrunching forward, she did the same to the second pair of prints. "Good, he's hurt," she said with a nod of her head. "I'll follow until where he enters this copse, and then find a place for the night." It made her feel better hearing her voice in the expansive buzzing silence. The plan made her feel better too. She set right off again after the limping footprints.

The sound of crashing branches stopped her short. No farther than a stone's throw away, the head of a giant tusked elephant suddenly appeared. Namelok froze and thanked Loitipitip and her father for teaching her about elephants. As he came out into the open, he was shaking his head as if he had a big bug in his ear and ramming his gleaming giant tusks into the ground.

Afraid even to breathe, she stood as still as the thorn-bush beside her. She hoped the metal jewelry dangling on her forehead wasn't glinting in the setting sun. The elephant continued to toss his head, this time reaching for the sky with his trunk. He blasted a trumpeting that set Namelok's frayed nerves into a silent frenzied scream. With a final head throw side to side, he settled down.

It was then that he realized that he wasn't alone. With his trunk still raised, he sniffed the air and turned to look directly at her. Namelok leaned into the thicket next to her and froze. She could see little spurts of blood where the thorns punctured her skin. The elephant let loose another angry loud trumpeting, lifted his head and ran straight at her. Namelok stayed glued to her spot, with a shadow of hope, for a lifted head usually meant a fake charge. The elephant charged, kicking up great clouds of dust around his huge feet as he ran at her. Then, as suddenly as he had started, he stopped. Just stopped, flapped his ears a few times, shrieked another loud blast from his trunk, then turned and walked casually away.

Namelok dropped to the ground when she could see him but no longer smell him. Sweat ran down from her headband, stinging her eyes. She thought her heart would burst through the front of her cloth.

The immense feeling of relief was joined with pride. She had stood her ground with an elephant. And won. Never, ever, had she been so close to Enkai's biggest creature. She had gazed at the giant animals from a distance and appreciated their beauty, but had always done her best to give the giant and powerful elephant lots of space. Now she had a story of her own to share with her father and brother.

"I wish *Papa-ai* was here right now," she said. "He would know how to pass the night." She wondered if he had gotten home yet from the Council of Elders. "Surely someone will go for him when I don't return home tonight." Her conversation of one forced her back into her immediate problem: how to spend the night safely. Tapping her fists, still sore from pounding the ground, on her thighs, she told herself, "Every animal that eats meat starts hunting at twilight." That was now.

She knew she would provide a tasty meal for a hungry lion or leopard, even the wild African dogs she had heard of but never seen. Her stomach clenched in fright, for never, not ever, had she been so alone in the bush on the brink of darkness. "I will survive," she said to the growing night. She hadn't eaten since sunrise, nor had a drop to drink, but that did not concern her now. Shelter for the night was the most important thing.

She looked around her and suddenly saw a lone acacia tree, across an open field of scrub grass and termite hills. It had a trunk larger than she could hug. Right away she knew that that would be her home for the night. It looked so alone, but it would protect her backside if she leaned against it the whole night. Sleep, she was sure, would not pass her way. Not that night. She looked at the sturdy tree and then back at the copse and knew what she would do. A look at the sinking sun told her she had better get started.

Namelok leaned down and grabbed as many thorn branches as she could. The longest one took a while to work loose, and she had almost given up when it suddenly broke free. As she dragged it from the bush, it grabbed another long branch and dragged it along. "That's what I'll do!" she said with the first bit of hope she'd felt all day. She pulled the second branch out and laid it opposite the first one, then took off her skin shoulder cloth and tied the four corners to the two branches. She was glad she had worn her longest skin that morning, for it covered more than half the length of the poles, making a sled like the one she had seen a sick old woman transported on.

Slowly but with a feeling of being in charge she piled thorn branches on the leather skin. She stacked them as high as her waist, then walked forward to see if she could lift the load. She grabbed the two branches like handles, hefting up the deadweight behind her. "You can take more," she commanded herself, and put it down and went to pick up more pieces.

She piled on more branches and bushes until she couldn't see over them. She walked to the front of the pile, shook loose her shoulders, bent and lifted up the sled of wood. The first step took all her willpower, for she was sure that if she could just get going, she would reach her tree. Dropping her head into her chest and letting loose with the most unladylike of grunts, she took the first step forward.

Her shoulders screamed, and her hands, already sore from beating the ground after finding the disgusting carcass of Emuny Narok, burned. Her breath sounded like *Yieyio* Emuny Narok's birthing breath. Like a slap, the thought reminded her all too quickly of why she was even in this situation. Was it true that only this afternoon she had found the saddest, most heartbreaking thing she'd ever seen in her life?

A picture of the mutilated head and single foot crossed her mind against her will, and enraged her and sent a flow of energy through her that she didn't know she had. With long steps she dragged her load forward. When she reached what she thought would be the boundary of her *enkang*, she dropped the sagging load and fell to the ground. On hands and knees she swallowed, gulped air and gasped. It was her shadow that brought her back to the task at hand, for it stretched long across the ground.

Jumping to her feet, she became aware of the variety of pains shooting through her body. "Later—I'll worry about this later," she said as she tried to ignore every screaming muscle and her cut-up arms and hands. "Just focus on building your *enkang*; that way you can finish quickly." Then she bent to her task.

She started just behind the tree, laying a circle of thorns that wound its way around the tree. She sat back against the trunk with legs out straight to see just how big to make the area between the end of the thorn wall and where she would sit against the tree. The first circle and half the second layer was completed when she ran out of thorn protectors. Looking to the west, she saw the sun begin its final dip toward the earth. Her heart shot to her mouth as she looked at the little shelter she had just built on the giant, sprawling plain. It was not enough. If she hurried, she could collect one more load and be on her way back before total darkness. She knew that the moon was nearly full, and that it would help her put the final touches on her *enkang*.

Even though each muscle seemed to cry when she picked up the handles of her sled, she marched back toward the copse. She ran a chant through her head, "Siri Aang, Siri Aang," to keep her anger stoked and her fatigue away. At the nearest border of the copse, she immediately started grabbing the biggest clumps of thorn bush that she could. Some were still firmly connected to the ground, but plenty were loose.

She piled the bushes on her leather and wood sled, repeating again and again, "Siri Aang, Siri Aang." She didn't realize she was crying until the first tears dripped onto her shoulder. She stared at the trails they made on her dusty skin, and said, "This, Our Secret, I do for you." She placed her hand on her heart. "I shall find the man who killed you and your mother and do something. What, I don't know yet, but something."

She was sure the baby was dead, and eaten so completely that not a trace remained of the little rhino. The thought of a dead Siri Aang brought another flood of tears to her eyes. She shook her head and said, "Why should you believe this promise when I failed you so badly on the first one? The promise to protect you." Showing herself no mercy, she spat out, "If I had kept that promise, you'd both still be alive."

Once again she gave in to the energy that her anger gave her, and dragged the sled back to her *enkang*. There weren't as many branches as on the first trip, but she managed to build a wall of three layers. As she admired her work, the sun bid the day good-bye and a warm, purple light led in the darkness. As the dusk light grew, she could see the glow of rising moonlight off to the east. She looked back at her *enkang* and suddenly realized that she had left no gatepost to enter. Picking out the point farthest from the tree, she pulled out a section of the thorny brush wall.

She started to enter when she thought of two things: she must urinate, if possible, before entering so she wouldn't have to venture out into the night beyond her short walls, and she needed rocks. Loitipitip had taught her that. Every good herder knew how to throw rocks. She took her leather off the branch frame before entering and tied two ends around her waist, leaving a pouch in front for her to put her rocks into. Fortunately the ground was pocked with many stones, big enough to throw at anything that frightened her. As the moon rose above the horizon, she worked quickly, looking both ways frequently as the night became brighter with the brilliant moonlight, for she felt too exposed. She walked into her tiny enclosure and dropped her stones. Then she went outside the gate and squatted to relieve herself. It was the eerie whooping call of the hyena that sent her scurrying into her *enkang*.

ONCE INSIDE, WITH legs stretched out and the thorn
walls closed in around her, Namelok took a long, deep
breath. She thought—no, she knew—that she had just
had the worst day of her life, to be followed by what
would surely be the longest night of her life. A day
worse even than seeing Loitipitip dance for the tourists.
As the shadows grew longer, she piled the stones near
her right hand, making a pattern to keep her mind busy.

"Right now Mother will be passing the bowl of
yogurt around to the sisters. Father is there if he has
returned," she said, "and I know that he is worried." She
could hear her mother sucking her teeth with concern,
then saying in a normal voice, "She'll be here soon, and
if she is not, we shall go look for her. She's fine, I am
sure, having a great conversation of one. She probably
doesn't even miss us like we miss her." Namelok was
sure her mother would drop her head and give way to a
shudder that shook her from head to toe. In her mind's
eye Namelok could see people running about, organiz-
ing groups to spread out over the plains in search of My
Sweetest One, who was out on the savannah in the dark,
alone.

And then, like a punch in her stomach she thought, Maybe not. Maybe they think I ran away from my own *emuratare*. That made her feel sick, for if there was one thing she wasn't, it was a coward. She had promised her mother that she would follow tradition. And her mother knew she was not a liar. With a sudden certainty she knew her mother would let all who were under the tree— was it really just three days ago?—know that she did not suspect her daughter of fleeing from her initiation.

"I will be fine," Namelok assured herself and the crickets. "I will fight the lion, scare the hippo, charge the buffalo and catch the poacher." That word, *poacher*, made the bile rise in her throat. She thought of Kakuta saying that the people who kill the rhinos and the elephants are the worst. She remembered him saying he would run a spear through the first poacher he caught, and she knew right away what she would do when she caught the killer. She would turn him over to Kakuta the Maasai. If she could see the poacher from a distance, maybe she could identify him and give Kakuta his name. If she didn't know him, she didn't know yet how she would capture a stranger. She would think of something, for she really meant to keep this new promise to the two dead rhinos. At least she had some plan again, and it made her feel better.

Her peaceful moment didn't last long, for from afar she heard the distinct grunt of a lion. It was a repeated *umph*, *umph* that rumbled from deep inside its stomach. To calm her own stomach filled with twitching nerves, she said, "The sound of a full lion." It was walking in her direction, and she imagined that each grunt represented a step closer to her.

Reaching deep inside, she said, "Enkai, you helped me find my friend Emuny Narok, although it was too late to save her, and helped me find the tracks. You helped me build my *enkang*. Now please help me survive the night." She knew that was the longest prayer she had ever made to Enkai, and breathed with relief when she heard the grunts turn away. The thorns would not have stopped the lion if it had kept coming and wanted her. She glanced skyward to give thanks and got another idea. Why not climb the tree?

There was a strong branch, running parallel to the ground, taller than her father's or brother's head. If she were up there, a lion would have to brave the thorns and climb the tree to get her. Also, the moon was so bright, she would watch the night pass and day arrive. If she fell asleep, she would start to fall, and fear of that would also help keep her awake all night. The lowest branch was within her grasp, and she leapt up to grab it. Her muscles, so tired from dragging the heavy branches, cramped as the full weight of her body dragged on them. She used her feet to climb up, like the monkeys she had watched, just like a game she had played with Loitipitip as a young herder.

A loud puff of breath preceded each step up the tree's trunk, until she finally flung her left leg over the first branch. When she looked down and realized how hard it had been to accomplish so little—for her feet were nearly touching the ground—she gave a little puff of indignation. Looking up, she said, "Now stand up on this branch and grab the one overhead."

Following her own directions, she slowly rose, hugging the trunk to her like she would hug her father and mother when she saw them again. The thought of them, worried and unhappy, filled her mind. A slight whimper escaped her mouth and she said, "Get moving." Her simple order gave her the spring she needed to stand upright. The distance to the next branch came to her shoulders. "Just pounce up there, like the leopard with its prey," she said to encourage herself. And like a monkey leaping branch to branch she lifted herself high and hung, belly down, over the branch.

With a final grunt and burst of energy she swung her legs around and sat astride the branch. Her cloth rode up her thighs, exposing much more leg than she usually did. She modestly pulled the cloth down, then laughed at herself and said, "Who is going to see this leg? I wish there was someone."

She sat, legs dangling over opposite sides of the branch, her back leaning against the trunk. The nearly full moon created a shadow garden, silhouetting smaller trees, termite hills, thornbushes and a giant hippo that suddenly appeared from behind a dense bush. Its head was down as it ripped sparse patches of grass from the ground. Namelok knew that water would not be too far away if a hippo was out grazing, for they spent their days by water. Maybe he would stay the whole night and lead her to water in the morning. One thing she knew for sure, all hippos are born in a bad, bad mood, so she was in the right place, up a tree.

She snuggled down against the trunk behind her. It was amazing how alive the night was. She saw the sloped-shoulder run of a pack of hyenas, loping along single file in the moonlight. And there was a family of grazing warthogs snuffling along in the moonlit savannah. The three babies frolicked around their parents, who had their snouts to the ground. Mother's tail rose straight up, a flagpole to her children. "Doesn't anybody sleep around here?" Namelok asked the African night. The last lingering notes of her voice floated on the air. She rested, her head propped against the trunk as she willed each and every muscle in her tired body to relax.

"I must sleep," she said to the night sky, "because tomorrow I will find the poacher who killed Emuny Narok, whoever he is."

She shivered, and as an afterthought added, "If nothing has me for dinner tonight."

SOMEWHERE AROUND DAWN, when a chill filled the air, the giraffes arrived. A tall stately male led a group of ten across the emerging plain, their long shadows cast by a falling moon preceding them. Stopping at an acacia tree not quite as tall as the one Namelok sat in, they started to browse. All except one. "A young male," she whispered to no one but herself. He was apart from the others, and rather than eating he was watching the lead male.

It was too early for Namelok to leave, and so in the early morning light, she watched. At first it looked like a stately, long-legged game of tag, like she had played a million times, as the young male made his challenge to the much bigger male. Standing on either side of an acacia tree, with very slow, deliberate steps, they walked tight circles around the tree. It was clear that neither trusted the other.

Each one slowed his stepping pace and stood absolutely still. "You've made a mistake, young friend," Namelok cried out to the challenging male, for his smaller size became obvious on the first pose.

As she watched the slow-motion fight start, she thought of her brother Loitipitip. Years before, when they ranged the plains together following their goat herd, they had watched a giraffe battle. Loitipitip had said, "The younger one will win. Youth is on his side." When the young giraffe departed in defeat, Namelok had turned to her brother. "I guess you were wrong. Don't challenge any warriors," she had said with a laugh. Loitipitip had laughed too, and then took off running to hide his embarrassment.

Looking at the young giraffe now, she called out, "You should avoid this challenge at all costs." But it was too late.

They stretched their long necks to the fullest extent, huge heads pointing their noses skyward, each watching the other. It was obvious that the dominant male stood another foot and a half taller than his challenger. It was also obvious that there could be only one winner in the building confrontation.

Never losing eye contact, they rearranged themselves so that they stood head to tail. Namelok watched enthralled as each swung his neck out and away, like a warrior cocking his arm back to send a spear flying. The heavy heads picked up momentum in their wide, arcing swings, and now with a force that surprised her and must have shocked the young giraffe, the big one landed a blow on the young challenger's chest, just above the breastbone. Namelok gasped with pain as the loud *thunk* of horns on chest carried across the plain between her tree and the giraffes.

"Oh," she blurted.

For more than an hour, as the sun climbed higher

into the sky, the two exchanged blows, keeping Namelok in her treehouse. Little breaks in the action gave each the opportunity to walk away, but neither did. Again the *thunk* of horns on skin echoed across the empty space, as the big one sent smashing blow after smashing blow to his opponent, leaving both Namelok and the young giraffe breathless. Finally, with a shake of his head, his neck hanging in defeat, the challenger moved off.

"Finally," Namelok said to the warming day, eager to pick up the tracks.

She climbed down from her roost that had begun to feel so safe, anxious to make up for lost time. Pulling the gate out of the thorn wall, she stepped out onto the open plains. She already missed the safety of the tree's branches, but shook herself. "You have a new promise to keep."

A troop of baboons passed by slowly, oblivious to her as the babies grabbed one another and rolled along, while smaller ones sat comfortably perched on their mothers' rumps, supported by tensed tails. The adults walked with a purpose, which reminded Namelok of hers.

She ripped some tree bark off and stuffed it into her mouth. Its rough surface grated against her tongue, but she kept it there because she knew it would fight hunger and quench her thirst. Loitipitip had taught her that too. But it wasn't enough. Through her bitter mouthful of bark she said, "Water. I need water."

The hippo! She could follow the hippo's path into

the copse. It would be dangerous. She didn't even know if the path went to the river, but she needed to find out. Her thirst was great. "What if there's a lion drinking?" she said, then scolded herself, saying, "Think the best. And think quiet."

"People are losing the power to be still," her father had told her long ago. He had looked so handsome that day with his long red and white bead earrings dangling from holes in the tops of his ears and swinging beneath the long empty loops of ear skin. His eyes shone as he talked way back then. "We must take lessons from the gazelles and the eland, the leopards and the crocodiles— from all of Enkai's wild animals, for they know the value and art of moving gently through the bush. One must blend with the sounds and the smells and the rhythms that surround them."

Her father's words echoing in her head made her feel stronger. Standing straighter, she said to the departing troop of baboons, "So that is what I shall do. I shall leave no path and disturb no stone, and I will be safe."

Namelok took a deep breath before entering the wide hippo path that disappeared around a bend inside the copse. She had no idea how long the trail was, or even if it went to the river. At least there are large shade pools to walk through, she thought for about one breath. "I am not the only thing that likes shade," she whispered, bending low and trying to crouch her way down the path. "Be the hippo," she told herself. "Be the lion." It took only six steps before she felt foolish and decided to walk straight and remember what she passed so she could return to the opening that would put her back on the trail of the poacher.

The buzz of her friends the cicadas, chirping away in a continuous high-pitched hum, reassured her. The path widened out about head height and she tried not to think of how high an elephant's sides are, for she suddenly realized that this must be the trail the elephant had emerged from yesterday. "Was it really only just yesterday?" she asked. So much had occurred. She'd been charged by an elephant, spent the night in a tree and watched a giraffe fight. And then came the flash of *Yieyio* Emuny Narok, a gory picture that filled her mind and heart and stoked her anger.

She picked up the pace, forgetting all of her father's advice and regretting it immediately as she stalked around a bend into a wide-open space and sent a herd of grazing wildebeest running in all directions. A young one stood bleating in the space, obviously separated from its mother. The beseeching bleat filled Namelok with guilt and dread. She knew the chances were good that the mother and baby would not meet again. If that happened, it would surely be someone's dinner soon. And it was all her fault for not following her father's words.

She froze, and tried to fit into her surroundings so the mother and baby could reunite. Her breathing was shallow and silent as she listened to the baby cry. The young wildebeest bleated and turned circles. He was very young, for his mane and beard were stubby, and a dried umbilical cord still dangled from its belly. He looked directly at Namelok, his brown nose and cheeks blending into a light brown forehead. The tiniest of horn nubs stuck out of his head.

A little sob escaped from My Sweetest One as she watched the panicked baby. Namelok felt like her heart was breaking, sad for the baby suddenly separated from its mother because of her, then sad for herself for the same reason. The young Maasai girl stood frozen in the morning sun, completely confused about what to do when a long bleating *mooooooo* filled the air. The baby whirled on its spindly legs and called back. It took off running just as its mother appeared. She trotted along, mooing plaintively until she saw her baby, and then the mother and young one charged to each another. They nuzzled upon meeting, then quickly ran off to join the herd.

A huge sigh of relief flowed from Namelok. "Oh, *Papa-ai*, if you were here, you would make me pay attention. But I will now, for it could have been much more dangerous." She shivered at the thought of surprising a lion or a hippo or buffalo. Before her nerve could fail her, she shook her shoulders, tapped her thighs and told herself, "Get going, girl."

Once again she set off, walking slowly but steadily across the open space where the wildebeest had been, then back into the dense, closed brush that surrounded the animal path. She followed the four-toed prints of a hippo that spread wider than her open hand along the trail. Cloven hoof tracks of gazelle and long two-toed prints of ostrich also filled the trail. But there was not a human footprint or rhino track to be seen.

"Oh, yes!" she suddenly blurted out. Right before her, standing alone on the ground was a spread of green leaves growing along a stem. Her stomach growled at the sight. She looked in all directions to see if any animals were heading her way, but saw none. She combed the ground for a stick to dig with, finding a small branch that forked into two strong sticks. She broke off a piece. It was pointed and strong, perfect for what she needed to do. Now hunger gripped her.

"Loitipitip," she said, "how many of these sweet squashes did we eat together?" She thought back again to their days of herding the grazing goats and sheep. If they weren't chasing game or resting in any shade they could find, they were searching for things to eat. Her lonely voice echoed in the morning sun, and she suddenly felt unbelievably alone. "I wish you and Father were here. You'd know how to catch the poacher when I finally find him."

She dropped to her knees next to the plant, talking all the while. She ripped the stick through one of the long, flat, thin green leaves. A milky juice oozed out. "Thank you, Enkai, for leading me to the right plant," she said. She knew for sure that the leaves were connected to the squash she wanted, growing underground.

She followed the long stem lined with leaves back to where it sprouted from the earth, crawling quickly on her hands and knees. She didn't know which hurt more, her hands and knees on the rough, uneven ground, or her empty belly. Taking her stick, she dug carefully around the stem. In her days with the warriors in their old home they had feasted many times on the *enkosikos*, and she remembered well all the techniques to extracting the squash. She dug with tight little jabs, working her way away from the stem, for everyone knew that if you cut the stem before seeing the squash, it would hide and you would never find it.

"Be patient," she said, "for every time you touch the squash before you get it out, it loses taste." And then she laughed at herself and said, "But how long has it been since you ate or drank? Just get the squash, foolish girl!"

She then began digging with hard chops at the ground. With a loud *snap!* her digging stick broke. The hunger that had only lurked on the edges before finding the squash plant twisted her empty stomach. She threw the broken end of the stick down and picked up another, fatter than the first one. "Slow down," she instructed herself. "Pay attention to your hand working and not to your stomach growling."

With a slow determination she worked away at the ground surrounding the root. Little bits of dirt flew up, and one piece lodged in her eye. She dropped the stick and wiped her filthy hands on her dirty skirt. Namelok reached up and pulled her eye open. Six flies flew off her face and she apologized to them, saying, "Sorry, ancestors, for disturbing you, but I need to clean this eye." All Maasai knew that flies were ancestors departed and let them gather as they liked, in eyes, on sores, wherever.

With a very soft swipe of her finger, Namelok felt the piece of grit move. Slowly, almost tenderly, she moved the grit to the corner of her eye. Satisfaction filled her as she pulled a little stone out, then stared at it perched upon her fingertip. She flicked it off, saying to herself, "Now pay attention."

With total concentration she dug. The stem reached down into the earth for almost a foot, and Namelok chopped the earth, then scraped away the dirt with her hands. At last she saw it, not much bigger than a large potato, a dirty brown color. She grabbed the squash from the hole, brushed the dirt from it, and plunged her stick into it to open it up. She sighed with delight at the sight of the fleshy white meat inside, then tipped the fruit over her mouth to catch every last drop of the sweet juice.

Still using her stick, she dug loose the white fiber inside and stuffed it into her mouth. She sighed again at the pure pleasure of liquid flowing down her throat and chunks of sweet, soft squash to swallow. She ate until there was absolutely nothing left in the skin of the squash, then sat back on her heels and slowly wiped her face. With slow deliberate swipes of her hand across her mouth she licked off every last drop and flavor of the squash. It didn't fill her empty stomach, but it definitely helped, both mentally and physically. "If I found it once," she announced to the singing crickets and the flock of hornbills flying overhead, "then I'll find more."

But now she looked up at the sun worriedly. The day was getting past her. She hadn't reached the river, which she still needed for her only slightly slackened thirst. Worse, she hadn't gotten back on the poacher's trail. She jumped to her feet and went back to the hippo trail she had followed there. Trying to gather her thoughts, she focused on being quiet. She needed to make up for all the time she had spent watching the giraffes, then scaring the wildebeest, then eating. It didn't register right away what she was seeing in front of her. When it did, she dropped to her knee for a closer look.

Sure enough, there, on the same trail, was the round toe print and the flat foot not far ahead, half hidden by one large hippo print. It was him—he may have needed water too. Fear filled her heart, for she still didn't know what she would do when she met him. She thought of Siri Aang and Emuny Narok, and anger pushed the fear aside. Namelok's eyes scoured the trail. Clearly the poacher had passed this way.

She crouched down close to the ground to make sure it was the poacher's track, and then she saw something that made her feel sick, for also passing along the very border of the path were the unmistakable prints of a baby black rhino. Then she was alive—Siri Aang was alive! She felt the blood pounding in her head.

But then she bolted upright. "Could it be? You, Beast," she snarled. She had already decided that she wouldn't call him a man anymore, preferring *poacher* for its evil sound. But now it had changed again, and *Beast* was the word she would use. "Not satisfied with killing the mother?" she said, choking on her disgust and anger.

Maybe it wasn't Siri Aang. Maybe it was another baby rhino. Her heartbreaking voice filled the air when she answered her own question. "No, I see no mother's prints along this trail." Placing a cupped hand over the tiny print shaped like a man's wide head with a big ear sticking out on each side, a tear splashed on the back of her hand. "It is you, Our Secret, because you fit nicely in the palm of my hand." She stood then, following the baby rhino spoor. How could she have missed the prints before? The Beast's footprints appeared now and again, down the middle of the path. Unless he had the baby rhino on a lead, he must have been following slowly behind with his injured foot. Then it occurred to her. By following the footprints of the poacher she might find Siri Aang again, alive.

Namelok followed both tracks on her hands and knees until she emerged onto the bank of the wide river that had game trails leading down to the water. The water sparkled in the sunlight, moving at a lazy pace because it was so shallow. Hippos lay along the bank, covered in a red ooze, their protection from the pounding rays of the sun. When she noticed that the sun stood directly overhead, she realized how long she had been in the copse. Frustrated at first, she relaxed because she was already on the trail of the poacher again, and would not have to return to where she entered the copse.

She picked the game trail that lay farthest from the hippos. It was steep and slippery, and she tripped down the last few feet, skidding to a stop at the water's edge. So many animals had passed through that she couldn't tell one track from another. "Water," she purred. Before bending down to drink, she searched the surface for traces of a submerged crocodile.

The fresh squash juice had helped her thirst, prying her dried tongue from the roof of her mouth, but the sight of so much water sent her to her knees to drink. She dipped her hands into the river, watching in all directions as she did so, then gulped down her first water in more than one full sun and one full moon. It slid down her throat with ease, and she rushed to fill her hands and then her mouth again and again, as quickly as she could. It relieved the ache in her throat and belly that the squash had helped, but not deadened.

Namelok splashed water over her head and across her face, then took her leather shoulder piece and submerged it into the river. She scrunched it up into a ball, trying not to squeeze any water out so maybe she would have some for later. She looked up at the sky and realized that the morning had passed. She needed to get going. Late afternoon would bring many thirsty animals to the river's banks, and she didn't want to be there when they arrived. And more than ever she needed to catch up with the poacher.

"Thank you, Enkai, for the food and the water," she said as she scrambled back up the game trail. She stopped at the top to watch a brilliant kingfisher bird flap its wings furiously above the water before diving in and darting below the surface. Just then a loud *eueow, eueow* filled the air. She looked overhead at a beautiful fish eagle, patrolling over the river. It threw back its white head and stretched its black wings wide, calling again, *eueow, eueow.* With one graceful swoop it skimmed the water, catching a large struggling fish in its talons. Namelok shook herself and said, "Get going. You're wasting time and daylight. Siri Aang needs you." She was glad she didn't have to retrace the path through the copse. She would follow Siri Aang's small prints until . . .

Namelok didn't want to think about what might lie at the end of the trail. A momentary picture of a dead Siri Aang flashed through her head like a lightning bolt, and stopped her dead in her tracks. It would kill her to see that, and for the first time she thought about giving up the search. Then she thought about the Beast escaping, and her anger fed her once again. "I will face what I must face," she told herself. "Because I will find the Beast and turn him over to Kakuta, who will spear him."

Her resolve was firm as she covered the area at the top of the path down to the water, looking for Siri Aang's prints that went away from the river, but still scared for the baby rhino's life. She feared she would never again see her little friend alive. A baby rhino with no mother stood little chance of surviving. Who would protect her? Namelok thought. What will she eat if not mother's milk?

She picked up the trail of the tiny rhino tracks at a marshy curve in the river, hugging her wet skin cloth to her stomach. The path was clear for a while; then scattered prints were visible at odd distances, as if the baby rhino had wandered on and off the path. Her back ached as she crouched along the trail, following the tracks.

When she stood to stretch out a growing kink in her back, she blurted, "What happened to the Beast? I haven't seen his prints in a long while." She turned left and right, searching the scorched earth. There were no traces of the limping foot or the full flat one. What could it mean? she wondered.

With a sudden glimmer of hope she called out to the buzzing cicadas, "Maybe he got eaten by a crocodile at the water's edge." The thought made her happy. If the poacher was dead, she wouldn't have to deal with him. And for as long as she could see Siri Aang's sporadic trail walking alone, she felt better. It meant the baby rhino was still alive.

23

THE AFTERNOON SUN sent Namelok's shadow before her. Small rivers of sweat ran down from her beaded headband. She was glad she was not wearing the tall beaded crossbar piece that dangled shiny silver triangles. In fact she had changed her headdress when she shaved her head the last time, only four mornings ago. The shiny pieces that hung down her forehead now stuck to her wet skin. Her layered beaded necklaces dipped with each step she took. Wiping the sweat from her brow, she rested for a moment and looked around.

Giant passing white clouds whisked the blue sky clean. Patches of short grass sprang up from the dried ground. An *Oreteti* tree in the distance looked so inviting that she was sure the baby rhino would head that way. It wasn't long before the tracks led her directly into the shadow's spill of the tree.

With a contented sigh she sat down. The hot afternoon, the long walk and the sleepless night all set upon her as she leaned back against the tree's trunk. "A small break," she told herself. "You need your strength for whatever lies ahead." Her eyes slowly closed and would have stayed that way if a sudden squabbling hadn't erupted over her head.

A large brown African kite was diving at an angry owl protecting its nest. He flew by, over and over again in large swoops, flying just above the squawking parent bird. The attacker's yellow beak swept closely over the screeching head of the mother owl. Namelok jumped to her feet, searched for a large rock and threw it at the marauding raptor. "Go away," she screamed, "I am sick of death and killing!" Emuny Narok's butchered head flashed before her eyes, and she gulped back giant tears that threatened to fall.

She couldn't believe she had almost fallen asleep in the middle of the day in the middle of the bush. She stood and looked long and hard in every direction. Heat waves danced where the sun was headed, and the watery sight of grazing zebras on the horizon greeted her to the west. A slow-moving herd of elephants ambled toward the river she had left hours ago. Mothers walked along with their heads down, babies running alongside, or just slowly drifting with the herd. The south held nothing but rolling sweeps of land, some with scattered grass but most as bald as an old Maasai woman's head. And to the north, the way the tracks led, were silhouette herds of wildebeest, zebra, something small, like gazelles, and one tall giraffe.

Namelok checked the sun and then squeezed the leather shoulder cloth she had dipped in the river over her head. She held her mouth open beneath it just in case one last drop could be forced out, but nothing came. She tried sucking on it, but it was dry and only made her homesick, for it tasted of smoke. She longed to be sitting in their dark, smoky hut, surrounded by Lankat and her parents. "Get going," she ordered herself. "Don't think about home, think about Siri Aang." And with that she continued her tracking.

For more than an hour, as the sun dipped toward the far horizon, Namelok followed the tiny tracks of Siri Aang. The trail ran dry when she entered a grassy area, for the grasses hid the tracks. She started walking in circles, bigger and bigger, out from the last print she had seen, hoping to sight another print when the grass gave way. It was on her third pass that she saw the track she dreaded.

She dropped to her knees and cried, "The Beast has been here." She traced the left footprint. He was definitely dragging that foot across the dirt, leaving a longer mark than before. Blood splatters dotted the print. "Good," she told the wounded footprint. "You must really be hurting." Anger filled her, and she swiped the footprints with her hand, wiping them out. "That's what I want to do to you," she shouted. Rage drove her to her feet, and she took off, following the poacher's tracks that led off to the west.

She searched for the baby rhino's prints, but there were none. With each hurrying step she took, she cursed the Beast. "Maybe Our Secret has lost you," she said to the human footprints, one dragging, one flat and full. Fear echoed in her voice as worry lines worked their way across her forehead. "Please, Enkai, let Siri Aang be far from the Beast." Choking on the words she didn't want to say, she whispered in spite of herself, "Please don't let Our Secret be dead."

She followed the poacher's tracks that led toward another stand of trees. Off in the distance to the west stood one tall thorn tree, a beautiful *Olchurai* tree, all by itself. Its branches spread wide, and its top was flat as if an elephant had sat on it. Namelok looked at the tree and the waning sun and decided that wherever the trail led, she would spend the night in that tree. This time she wouldn't bother dragging branches around to make an *enkang* wall, which was lucky because her strength was waning. Hunger and thirst tugged at her mind, while fear and rage filled her thoughts.

24

IT SEEMED LIKE it took forever to get to the tree. She left a pile of stones where she departed from the prints, eager to get settled before sunset. The tree she had chosen had branches laden with thorns, and she needed all the light she could get to avoid piercing herself on one. Each broad thorn tapered down to a sharp, pointed weapon.

She dropped to the ground next to the trunk to contemplate climbing the tree. Having a plan, no matter how meager, made her feel better. She knew that now. Namelok stretched out to lean back on her elbows, staring up at the tree, trying to decide exactly which of the lower branches looked the easiest to get to. All she knew for sure was that, easy or hard, she would climb the tree before the sun set.

A wide canopy of horizontal branches spread out from where the trunk divided into three separate branches that branched again and again into a giant umbrella. Peacefully she contemplated the beautiful *Olchurai* tree, then snapped back to attention. "Quit daydreaming unless you want to spend the night right where you are!"

As she stared skyward, she suddenly felt that she was

not alone. She actually saw the group before she heard them. They were each moving silently on four giant hoofed feet, munching on the treetop that was giving her shade. Brown star splashes covered their tawny bodies. Tilting her head back, she looked at the nearest one, not even a short stone's throw from her. She was sitting at toenail level, afraid to move, not because she feared for her safety, but because she didn't want them to leave. She needed some company, especially from animals that didn't eat meat.

Peacefully they steadily browsed nearer and nearer to her, seven giraffes munching their dinner. The largest female suddenly stopped. Her long silky eyelashes fluttered quickly as she looked at Namelok intently. She was so close to the young Maasai girl that she could smell the newly eaten leaves on the giraffe's breath. Namelok didn't move, and the giraffe fluttered her long lashes a final time and went back to eating.

Soon the smallest giraffe wandered her way. He was about seven feet tall, not much bigger than his birth size. Namelok watched silently as he headed toward her. He reminded her of a little boy, looking for some fun. His step was playful, and he looked fearless. Step by dancing step he moved closer to Namelok, whose eyes were wide and mouth was open. A ragged *nnuhh* snort came from the biggest female, the first sound she'd ever heard from a giraffe, aside from horns hitting skin. The young giraffe stopped in his tracks. He looked down his nose at Namelok, and then walked slowly around her and back to his mother.

Namelok sat frozen, a memory searing her brain. "You did the same thing, Siri Aang." Her eyes filled with tears as she quickly relived the day her sister rhino came the closest to her. She had been sitting on the ground, digging out an *enkosikos* squash, when Our Secret wandered her way. It was the day she learned her rhino pose—the day she knew being close to the ground was less threatening. Thinking of her close moment with the baby rhino wrenched her heart as she whispered to the young giraffe, "You animals are all alike. Emuny Narok gave Siri Aang the same 'get back here!' signal your mother gave you."

Namelok watched the mother giraffe as she bent her long neck, gently placing her forehead next to her baby's, and resting her long head along his neck. Namelok was touched by the tenderness, then caught her breath. "That too," she whispered. It was like Emuny Narok tenderly scraping mud off her baby Siri Aang. It was just the same.

When the giraffes finally wandered off far enough for Namelok to move, the sun was setting. She shook herself to get moving, for she needed the light to climb the tree. She noticed the young giraffe stretching his neck down to a small shrub. When he stood straight again and followed the herd, she rushed over to the shrub. Sure enough, there were the small red *irmankula* berries she hoped for. Running out of time as the sunset colors swept across the sky, she ripped off a single branch and ran back to the tree. They wouldn't kill the hunger that was once again building, but they would help.

She squatted at the foot of the tree to urinate, but nothing came. She tied her dried leather skin over her shoulder into a sling and placed the branch with its dangling red berries into it, then jumped up to look for the nearest branch. The lower branches had no thorns, which made it easier for starting her climb. Glancing up, she plotted her course from branch to branch. "I need a thorny area for protection so that maybe I can sleep a little," she said, jumping up. Grabbing the lowest branch, she felt every muscle ache and her hands that had had a day's rest burn like fire at the shock of grabbing the rough limb. Slowly she pulled herself up.

Sitting just below the spread of leafy branches, she checked to make sure that where she sat was clear of thorns. She leaned back gratefully against the trunk to let her muscles and hands recover briefly before continuing her climb. She couldn't remember ever feeling so tired in her twelve years. It was hard to know what was worse: her hunger, her aches and pain, her thirst or her fear of another night alone in the African bush. She knew what was strongest, and that was her determination to catch the Beast.

Moving as slowly as a chameleon, she hefted herself over the next branch that rested in the spiny protection of the tree's canopy. Carefully she broke off the sharp thorns hanging near her head, then, with a giant sigh, she leaned back against the trunk, settled for the night. Sleep, she thought. I need to sleep. And with that she drifted off before the sun had completely set, setting the sky aflame with orange and red and golden streaks.

When the moon began its downward arc in the sky, Namelok awakened, stiff and disoriented. She looked down upon a porcupine busily digging at the tree's roots for a snack. The clicking needles sent a gentle sound out into a night with its huge moon and flat plains with small hills scattered about. Namelok watched the black and white needles of the porcupine flop back and forth. She sat as quietly as she could, trying not to frighten it, for the last thing she needed was a foot full of porcupine quills.

Her stomach growled, announcing her hunger pains once again. She unslung the skin cloth hanging from her neck and started picking off the berries. Each had a hard skin that she squeezed between her thumb and finger, releasing a tasty sweet berry inside. She ate without stopping until a great thirst overtook her. The berries, so sweet, carried a strong aftertaste that dried the tongue and mouth. In a loud whisper she said, "Thank you, Enkai, for the berries, and for this tree that will quench my thirst." She ripped a piece of fresh bark off her perch and slowly chewed as she watched the African night.

"The night is as busy as the day," she said to the moon. She shivered as the long cackling laugh of a hyena call cut across the silence. Lion roars from a great distance echoed across the land and sent goose bumps racing up and down her arms. Feeling a little safe in her tree, she settled back for the rest of the night. "If something is going to get me up here, I'd rather not know about it in advance." And with that, she fell back into a light slumber.

She woke suddenly. Daybreak was well upon her. The sun sent glinting golden rays her way, promising a hot day. Dust devils spun in the distance, sending red clouds of dust high into the air. Namelok checked the sky for vultures, remembering with a punch that Siri Aang's footprints had disappeared. No vultures circled over any particular spot, which made her feel hopeful. Just maybe, although her tracks had disappeared, Siri Aang was still alive.

Looking north, south, east and west, she gasped over the beautiful morning. Seven giraffes were tall specks on the horizon, eating from trees. She was sure they were her friends from the day before and was glad to see them again. *"Ilmeuti,"* she called to the giraffes, *"supa!"*

It felt so good to greet the giraffes that she turned to the eland, such big and beautiful animals, able to leap higher than her father's head, grazing peacefully. *"Isiruai,"* she said, *"supa!"* Not a single eland looked her way to return the greeting. Once she started, she greeted everything in sight: the buffalo and birds, the elephants and warthogs, the graceful impalas leaping and the grazing zebras. Looking around again, she said to herself, "And look what they are all doing—eating."

Dropping from the tree, she ran over to the *irmankula* bush and filled her leather sling with the bright red berries. Just to be safe, she also ripped more bark off the *Olchurai* tree and placed it next to the berries. She didn't take time to eat, for the day was fresh and she wanted to get back on the trail of the Beast. What she wanted even more was to find the trail of Siri Aang once again.

As she strode along, Namelok thought of home. There would be no family breakfast of porridge made from maize meal, water and a little fresh milk, or crouching around the cow-dung fire inside the hut and chatting. She was sure her father was with the men and warriors, telling what people to go where in search of his daughter. Surely, after two nights of her being missing, chaos would own the *enkang*.

SLINGING HER SKIN full of berries and bark over her shoulder, Namelok marched over to the pile of rocks that marked the trail. The sun was just beginning to get a grip on the chill of the early morning air. She walked silently but quickly, trying to make up for some of the time she'd lost yesterday. She walked along with her eyes glued to the ground, hoping against hope to see Siri Aang's tiny tracks once again. In the morning stillness she followed the prints of the dragging left foot and flat right one. "I'll get you," she swore to the footprints. "I promised to catch you and I will."

She touched the flat footprint, then smacked it hard with her fist. She trudged along, never taking her eyes off the ground. Suddenly a troop of baboons began screaming, *sca-reeeech, sca-reeeech*, filling the air as they scurried across the dried earth. Namelok's heart raced in her hollow chest. She quickly looked over her shoulders, right then left, but didn't see what had sent the baboons running for their lives. Scanning the bush in front of her, she suddenly saw it. The unexpected appearance of the lion nearly sent Namelok crashing to the ground with fright so strong, she couldn't move. She froze. The lion had leapt up from behind a scrubby bush, covered in blood, her sides bulging.

Namelok stared at the angry four-hundred-pound lioness that was poised and roaring at her from a short stone's toss. Her roar made Namelok's ears ring, and the smelly breath of rotten meat pouring from her mouth almost made the young Maasai girl faint. Just when Namelok's heartbeat began to calm, the lioness roared. Again. Her head was huge, and she twisted it from side to side with each deafening *roarrrrrrr!*

Her appearance of pure muscle and raw power was almost diminished by the tremendous sound she let loose. Her bulging sides and bloody face let Namelok know that she probably wasn't hungry, in fact had just come from a kill. Hope popped into her mind for a fleeting second. Maybe the lioness had eaten the Beast! Namelok knew she had to do everything in her power to pose no threat. She had to wait as long as she could for the lioness to go away.

Another *roarrrrrrrr* shattered the stillness of the African morning, as well as Namelok's nerves. She wavered slightly as she felt fear shoot clear to the marrow of her bones. She knew who was in charge, and it wasn't Namelok, for her slightest movement sent the lioness roaring again. Now she stood as still as a tree. She tried to think of every story she had heard from the Elders and the *ilmurani*, even from proud mothers of lion hunters, about lion encounters. She couldn't think of a single story—not one. The only thing she knew to do was freeze.

Coming face-to-face with a lion was every warrior's dream. She could remember no advice about how to get away, because no warrior would want to. And no warrior would be this far from everywhere and everyone else in Enkai's world without a spear, she thought. In that moment the lioness sat down. She stretched her front legs forward and began to lick clean her mighty paws covered in blood. Namelok decided to try a few silent and slow steps backward since the lioness was so busy. It didn't take long to realize that it was a mistake, for in one fluid motion the lioness was on her feet again, matching the young Maasai girl step for step. Namelok was trapped.

With each step the lioness moved forward, she snarled and growled her displeasure. And so Namelok froze. Again. She felt her pounding heart from her toes to her eyes, and was sure that the lioness could hear the pulsing beats. The lioness's muscles rippled beneath her tawny skin as she jutted her head forward and showed her teeth. The ripple flowed from her shoulders to her sides, and down to her mighty haunches. Then she sat again with a gracefulness Namelok knew no human could match.

Namelok felt every nerve in her body, scared and thrilled at the same time. Frozen in place and breathing in shallow little gasps, she waited for the lioness to settle comfortably, then started her silent retreat in reverse again. With one smooth motion the lioness jumped up. Namelok froze again. My Sweetest One's legs trembled from fatigue and tension, and she knew that if she didn't sit soon, she would surely collapse.

The lioness toyed with her while the sun moved from east to west, rising and growing stronger as it did. Namelok focused on the big cat's full belly, telling herself she couldn't be hungry, that she had just eaten. Then a terrible thought popped into her head and she forced it away. Maybe this lion had eaten Siri Aang. Just as Namelok's leg muscles started to quiver with the tension of standing still for so long, the lioness flicked her tail and turned. It was not a moment too soon, for the girl needed to move to keep her legs working. She shook each leg quickly while the lioness wasn't looking.

A stand of scrubby bushes stood nearby and in one moment the angry lioness, bigger than life, disappeared behind it before Namelok's eyes. Sitting behind the bush, the lioness was hidden, but still very present. She continued to fill the air with disgruntled growls.

Slowly and deliberately Namelok walked backward, holding her breath and covering the shiny bangles dangling on her forehead. When she could no longer hear the grunts of the lioness, she broke into a run, heading for the nearest tree to climb. When she reached it, she tried to scramble up but only managed to fall to the ground. Gulping great breaths of air, and shaking from head to toe, Namelok looked over her shoulder to see if the lioness would appear again, ready for another round. But there was no sign of her. At the base of the tree she wept with relief and exhaustion and fear. Namelok felt even more tired than she had the night before.

When her heart stopped racing and her breathing slowed down nearly to a normal pace, she looked around her. She could see the troop of baboons playing now, grooming and resting in the bright sunlight. The biggest baboon stretched out on the ground as two females picked ticks from his broad back. "The lioness must be gone," she whispered to the relaxing troop. "Thanks for warning me it was there, and thank you, Enkai, for letting me live.

"Take a rest," she told herself. "You have had a busy morning." She pulled some berries from her sling and squeezed them open. As she thought about getting back onto the trail, she ate. Chewing made her feel good. It was an everyday thing in her crazy new life full of dangers and surprises. Bending over, she picked up a black stick, not as tall as her brother's spear, but of a good weight that felt sturdy. She hefted it like a spear, then walked with it as a support.

She had forgotten just how tired and achy she was in the rush of adrenaline that followed the meeting with the lioness. It was when she took a little weight off her legs by leaning on the stick that she felt the exhaustion. She looked up at the sun. She needed to get moving. It didn't take long to get back to the pile of rocks and pick up the Beast's footprints again. She walked into the hot afternoon sun, following the footprints while examining every inch of the ground. There were still no signs of Siri Aang. She didn't know if that was good or bad. "Please don't be dead, Our Secret," she said to an afternoon filled with the cooing calls of wood doves.

Looking around her once again, happy not to see the lioness, she said, "I've never been so deep into the park before. That's why I am meeting so many animals." Then she got back to her promise of tracking the poacher. She followed the smudge of the injured foot until stopping suddenly. She looked around her quickly, certain that she had heard her father's voice say, "The Maasai are the friends and protectors of all wild animals." She couldn't help but wonder if that's why nothing had attacked her.

Letting go a deep sigh, she said to the shimmering heat bouncing off the horizon, "Thanks for reminding me, *Papa-ai*. I wish you were here with me."

chapter

26

WALKING WITH HER black stick, Namelok followed the Beast's track as the sun followed its own path across the sky. Her shadow was now falling behind her, so she knew she had changed direction again. One thing was certain, she had no idea anymore which direction her *enkang* was. She stopped to look around the horizon, and that's when she saw it. A reddish-brown clump leaning back against a large termite hill. She knew right away what she was looking at—the man turned poacher turned Beast. She was thankful for her stick, as she felt it gave her some protection. The lump still sat motionless, so she decided to walk around and approach it from the back. Walking with deliberate steps, she crept up on the termite hill from behind, her stick held high, ready to strike. Her foot skidded on a small rock, and the lump's head turned.

It was impossible to know who was more shocked—Namelok or her father.

HE WAS TIRED and dirty as she had never seen him before. A wave of disgust rushed over her, something she never ever thought she would feel for her own father. For *Papa-ai*. Dried blood was caked on his *shuka* and on his foot, which was covered by flies. She gulped back a big swallow of bile shooting up her throat as he dropped his head in shame and closed his eyes tightly. With total disrespect and mocking in her voice she nearly choked on the words, "The Maasai are the friends and protectors of all wild animals?"

He opened his eyes slowly, and lifted his head. Her eyes showed such hurt and shock and disgust that he dropped his head in a shame beyond his worst imaginings. "Namelok-ai, what are you doing here?" he asked harshly, as if he belonged there and she didn't. She looked at his torn *shuka* and swollen foot and felt no pity.

In a voice just as harsh she said, "No, Father, what are you doing here?" Her eyes lingered on his bloody *shuka*.

"By the power of Enkai, believe me now. I am not a poacher, only their tracker. Both are bad, like a drought, but that is the truth as it is."

Namelok walked in circles. With only one *enkosikos*

squash, berries and bark in her belly, her necklaces, looser after two days, clicked as she stamped about. She flung to the ground her leather sling that still held a few berries on a branch and looked again at her father. Her heart almost softened a tiny notch toward the pitiful shadow of Reteti. Then she thought of Emuny Narok, butchered on the plains, and the missing baby. Her heart hardened again. He may not have sent the bullets flying, but he had, by his own admission, led the poachers to the rhinos. Her shock rocked her to the pit of her empty stomach—her own father had done such a thing.

"Both are bad?" she shrieked. "*Only bad* is what you call butchering a mother rhino? What do you call sending her helpless baby to its death? Then tracking it like a lion after its prey?" Bile filled her throat. "How, Father? How is this possible?" She shook her head, not believing what she was seeing. "Why, Father?" she cried. "Why?"

Reteti waved his arms at her, signaling her to be quiet. She couldn't believe it when the trace of a smile crossed his face. She felt a huge urge to slap him, her own papa, for that smile. He slowly rose to his feet, wincing, keeping his swollen and fly-covered heel off the ground. She could see that his sandal was hooked onto his heel, instead of flapping like it should. A mess of sticky blood oozed from around a giant thorn running straight through his thin leather sandal sole directly into his foot.

Ignoring his wound, he pressed his fingers to his lips, shushing his angry daughter. He limped ahead, not anything like the man she knew and loved. He was only a very old-looking man. With a flick of his hand he signaled her to follow him, then limped into a thick copse of bush.

She followed reluctantly, then whispered in a voice that surprised both of them, "Siri Aang, Our Secret!" For there the little rhino stood, alone, bewildered, but alive. Namelok couldn't take her eyes off the sad-looking baby. She couldn't stifle the smile that crossed her face at finding Our Secret alive. With a quick glimpse she looked at her father and said, "But why? How?" then dropped to the ground.

Her father stared at her, then whispered, "For nearly three days I have followed. Sometimes she wandered off to browse while I stayed on the open land, but she never left my sight. Even with a distance between us we stayed together. She walks slowly and so do I." They both glanced at his foot, the heel covered in blood over a thick callus that was nearly four decades old. A bottle-green shimmer of flies in the slanting sunlight crawled over his foot. She wanted to flick them away, but knew it was forbidden. She shuddered, then looked again at the baby rhino.

Forcing her eyes to look her father's way, she pointed at his foot. "Does it hurt?" she asked, still overwhelmed by her shock at finding her own father at the end of the trail, and happiness at seeing Siri Aang again—alive.

"Yes, it hurts, but nothing like the pain in my heart right now and my shame."

Looking over at the baby rhino, he said, "I have

followed it to protect it. It's very strange, for she does not run from the scent of a human." He looked at his daughter.

As they watched the baby rhino browse, a breeze came up and carried the girl's scent to it. Siri Aang's head lifted and her nostrils twitched. No anger or aggression appeared; in fact it almost looked as though relief swept over the tiny black rhino.

Namelok sent a low "currrr, currrr" out to the rhino, whose head snapped up as if she had been stung by a bee. With total amazement, Reteti watched his daughter and the baby rhino as Namelok crouched low, purring a gentle "currrr, currrr" to the rhino that walked toward her.

In a whisper, Reteti asked her, "When did you befriend a baby black rhino?"

Still facing Our Secret, Namelok said over her shoulder, "We can talk about that later. Now I want to walk toward that large *Olchurai* tree where we can spend the night." She chanced a quick look back at Reteti, not wanting to lose her contact with Siri Aang. "I will see if I can get her to follow me. If she does, then you can follow behind us." Slowly Namelok stood.

chapter

28

THE THREE MADE a strange sight on the horizon for the grazing zebras and the herd of ostrich, two males followed by eleven juveniles. First walked a tall, proud young woman, lips pursed and leaving a trail of soft "currrr, currrrs" in her wake. Behind her clomped a baby rhino, so small on the great plain and looking so old already. Then behind them both limped the tall man, leaning on the stick Namelok had dropped, his dirty red *shuka* hanging off his left shoulder, his *oringa* bouncing against his left thigh.

The sun's lower rim was balanced on the horizon when the three reached the tree. It was bigger than she expected, with its branches reaching far to the east and west, north and south, sending a large dark pool of shade across the ground.

Other Maasai travelers had been here before them. Traces of an old fire in a large stone circle remained, and a large flat stone for sharpening knives and spears lay at the base of the tree. It made Namelok feel more comfortable knowing that the tree had served warriors before them, though she knew not who or when.

Her father looked around approvingly. The tree was like an old friend, the biggest acacia in sight, surrounded by flat, barren plains, its branches filled with birds. Reteti sat at the base of the trunk and put his hand on its warm bark. "Thank you, Enkai, for this tree. And thank you for my daughter who led us here, a young woman of many surprises." He dropped his head as tears crept to the edges of his red-rimmed eyes.

"Can I tell you how I got here?" he was surprised to hear himself ask.

"Later," she said. "Right now we need to prepare for the night. Can you climb that tree?" There were many answers she needed. And she would make sure she got them.

Her father looked at her with his head to one side, then glanced at the tree. "I can climb, but do we need to?" He pulled up his snuffbox, a beautiful deep black piece of buffalo horn that had been rubbed smooth and bright with years of use. He tapped the small, snug-fitting leather cap. Decorated with red and white triangles separated by single rows of blue beads, a red and a green line of beads finished off the top.

Rolling it slowly between his hands, he said, "Why not build a fire instead? I didn't before because I was sure that the little one, what do you call her, would run away. But now that you're here, I'm sure she'll stay."

"Siri Aang is her name," Namelok said shortly. Suddenly she remembered why they were there and her anger flared again. "You remember her mother, the one that is dead? I called her *Yieyio* Emuny Narok, and we were a family."

She shook her head. She knew that if she kept going,

she would cry, and scream, and maybe even beat on her father's chest with anger and sadness and exhaustion and hunger—and total and complete frustration. This was the man turned Beast whom she had followed for two days. The Beast she had sworn to have arrested and disgraced. Even speared! Her beautiful father! She looked at him. He had dropped his head again, and she felt the slightest twinge of shame at her own cruel thoughts.

"We can talk tonight, *Papa-ai*."

He raised his head at the *ai*. It showed that she still recognized him as her father. Still claimed him as her father. In a high, soft voice that sent waves of respect toward his daughter, he replied, "*Aaa*, yes, Namelok-ai, we shall do as you say." Then he sighed wearily.

As her father settled against the massive tree trunk, she scoured the area for fallen branches, something good for digging roots. She had chosen the mighty acacia, the biggest she had ever seen, because she knew it would give them shade, and shelter and medicine for his foot. She was happier when she saw the small patches of short bushes growing in the shade of the tree. Already Siri Aang happily browsed at the edge of the shade there, near them but definitely apart. It was clear that the small rhino was learning to browse on her own, for she ripped little ragged chunks of leaves from the bush and dropped them before she could work them into her mouth.

So many questions hung in the air as she worked, like the dangling nests of the red and black weaver birds that flitted around them. One hung heavier. Why her father had done this—something so out of character. She just could not understand.

Reteti was watching Namelok as she gathered wood for the fire when he suddenly said, "You must have spent one or two nights alone in the bush. Few warriors, armed with spears, do such a thing." He shook his head in the dwindling daylight, overwhelmed with emotion.

Clearing his throat, he said, "Go to that *endorko* tree just over there, the one with the heart-shaped leaves, and find a dry branch on the ground, big enough to split in half. Also, pick a stick as long as your arm, as straight and slender as possible. Bring them to me."

Namelok strode over to the *endorko* tree and picked up a dry branch, as thick as her wrist. She kicked at a pile of sticks until she saw the one she wanted. It was long and smooth and felt good when she rotated it between her palms. She carried the two pieces of wood back to her father.

Trying to impress him with her knowledge, she said, "I'll find some dried zebra dung, or maybe a warthog's." The sun was racing toward the horizon so she hurried to find the dung that would catch the spark. She dropped the dried droppings beside her father, who was splitting the thicker wood with a sharp stone. As he laid it open flat, she returned with a handful of small twigs and grass.

Her father pointed at the split wood and said, "Shred the dung and place it under this *enyoore*. It would also help if you could hold the *enyoore* in place while I work for the spark."

She took two sticks and placed one on each end of the split branch while her father took the long slender stick and rolled it back and forth between his hands. "You have picked a fine *olpiron* stick for starting the fire, My Sweetest One. As soon as the sparks fly and the dung sends up a trail of smoke, remove the *enyoore* and I'll place the grass and twigs on top."

Neither spoke as Reteti placed the *olpiron* directly on the *enyoore* and slowly began to spin the wooden stick between his palms. His breathing became loud as he rotated the stick between his hands faster and faster, pressed firmly against the flattened branch. Namelok concentrated on holding the rubbing surface in place. The friction of the *olpiron* on the *enyoore* finally sent up a slender shaft of smoke. A spark jumped from the wooden *enyoore* to the dung, and more smoke rose. Quickly, Namelok removed the *enyoore* and Reteti dropped a handful of dried grass on the smoldering dung, then blew on it until the first delicate flames licked the darkness that was fast approaching.

As the sun's shadows grew longer, Reteti fed the fire. He used a small branch to act as their taper, lighting even smaller pieces piled high around the dung. Namelok couldn't believe how good it made her feel to hear the crackling of the flames as the branches caught and her father added bigger pieces to keep it all going. The growing fire warmed the evening air, but Namelok's heart remained cold from the shock she had received that day.

The Beast was her father. She could not understand.

29

NAMELOK BROKE THE silence that stood between her and her father when she dropped an armload of small branches into the old fire ring. She turned and picked up a pile of larger pieces, and laid them more gently to the side. Her emotions were running wild, but calmed down each time she looked over at the browsing baby rhino in the flickering firelight.

Her father glanced up over his shoulder at the spreading branches of the tree, then asked, "Is that how you have survived? Sleeping in trees?"

She wasn't ready to talk about her experiences yet, so she ignored his question and asked her own. "What have you eaten all these days?"

"Some berries, but mainly I chewed on the acacia bark to quiet my hunger and kill my thirst. The grass is good to make the saliva run, so I did that too. And what about you, my daughter?"

"One *enkosikos*, some berries and some bark." Her answer was short and he left it at that.

By the time the sun had set and the evening surrounded them, she said, "Let's take a look at your foot." The orange flames of the fire sent her shadow dancing behind her as she rose to sit closer to her father.

She had never really seen her father sick or injured before, but she was sure that even if his wound hurt badly, he would never complain. She raised his foot in the firelight and examined the large thorn sticking out of his heel. She knew it had to be removed. There was a thin red line running up the back of his foot, just visible above the dried blood. It alarmed her, for she knew that it meant a sickness inside was moving, spreading out.

She wasn't sure how to approach the problem when her father said, as if reading her mind, "I have an idea. Make your medicine first, and then I'll show you."

Namelok accepted his advice silently, digging in the darkness at the roots of the tree where a porcupine had been. Everyone knew that the roots of the acacia were very powerful. She mashed them on the sharpening stone with a rock, then went over and picked a small handful of grass and began chewing it slowly, making saliva. She spit into the sticky white sap that the root released. When she had a salve that was spreadable, she looked to her father for the next step.

"Place your medicine on the wound first, to see if it will loosen the skin's grip," he said. "I tried to pull the thorn out yesterday, but it broke off."

Carefully she plopped some of the white medicine into her palm. It was difficult to see what she was doing in the darkness that was only faintly illuminated by the fire. Watching her step, she carried the medicine over to her father's side. With a small stick she had cleaned earlier, she carefully spread the sap onto his wound, between the sole of the shoe and the sole of his foot.

Her father picked up his *oringa* stick and put the skinnier handle end between his foot and his shoe. "Take the ends," he said. "This way you don't have to touch the foot or the thorn, for if you pull and I hold my foot steady, maybe you can pull shoe and thorn out at once."

With reluctance she grabbed the ends of his *oringa*. It was like taking his hands in hers, for he had held and swung and rubbed and loved this *oringa* for longer than Namelok's twelve years.

She looked directly into his eyes. She noticed that something had changed between them. He was talking to her as if she were an adult. Maybe even a friend. They were two people working together to solve a problem. "Are you sure there isn't a better way to do this? It could be very painful."

He shook his head no. "This is best, but I don't know if we should do it fast or slow. I don't want to break a piece off inside."

"Let's start slow," she said. "If it is coming easily, then we can do it faster." She rearranged her knees that were tucked up under her. "You must stop me if it's too much," she told him.

"Enkai, please be with us," he whispered into the night as he wrapped his hands around his ankle. With a quick nod of his head, he signaled Namelok to begin.

Namelok looked skyward to the Supreme Deity, asking her for help just as her father had. With a deep breath she leaned back slowly to stretch out her arms for better control. She looked into the eyes of her father, and then she pulled ever so slightly. Nothing happened at first. She shook her head to stop a slow trickle of sweat that was running down from her headband toward her eyes. She pulled again, and ever so slowly there was movement. It felt like a gourd she had lifted from a spill of honey one time. At first the gourd had clung to the sticky mess, then slowly but surely it had broken free. It felt as if the thorn was looser, so she looked at her father, who once again gave a quick nod, and she pulled the rest of the giant thorn free.

Blood lost no time squirting out of the hole it had made. Namelok was glad she had waited till darkness to work because all the flies were gone. She winced for her father when she looked more closely at the wound in the firelight. What looked like a deep black hole was surrounded by caked blood and dirt. With a small stick she scraped as much of the mess as she could from her father's heel. She shook her head in wonderment when it occurred to her that she was cleaning the foot of the Beast she had pursued in rage.

Blowing out a breath to clear her head, she said as she worked, "Water would be nice to have to wash away this sticky mess." When she had cleaned it as well as she could, she flipped the stick around and used the other clean end to put more sap on the wound. It must have hurt very much, but her father did not say a word.

Namelok leaned over to the smooth stone where she had left a pile of leaves. She crushed them together, forming a solid mass that she placed over the medicine.

Using her beautiful straight teeth as a tool, she ripped a long leather strip off of her shoulder piece, then tied the leaf mass in place with the leather strand.

Reteti nodded his head in acknowledgment of her work well done, then said, "My Sweetest One, you will make someone a very fine wife, and be a very good mother one day."

Namelok rolled her eyes up from what she was doing and glared at her father. He held up his hand and nodded his head. "I speak only the truth."

Namelok leaned back on her feet and said, "Fine. So, *Papa-ai*, tell me the truth about how we got here."

A SUDDEN *SNAP!* filled the air as a dried piece of wood exploded in the fire. A shower of sparks, glowing bright orange in the dark night, shot toward the lower branches of the giant *Oreteti* tree they sat beneath. Namelok was glad that Siri Aang slept, undisturbed by the noise or the fire.

Reteti cleared his throat once, then again. Namelok could feel his nervousness, but she said nothing, for she wanted answers.

Shifting his weight from left to right and clearing his throat once more, her father finally began. "Five sunrises ago brought what I thought was the worst day of my life. And then I saw you today and my shame was so great that I could not lift my head. Perhaps if I talk the truth, it will help us both."

Namelok thought of the last story he had told her, about Enkai making all cattle for the Maasai. About Maasai being the protectors of all animals. How many lifetimes had passed since that evening? Was it really only weeks ago? She could feel an edge in her father's voice as he began. He was not telling her a traditional story. Those always made him feel proud. He was confessing, and his voice had a little shake to it that Namelok knew she had never heard before.

"I will make no excuses, but I will tell you of the cause. And the lowest point in my life. It all started when we left our traditional land and family and my oldest son. All my children were hungry—and my cattle were skinny, and the land not strong enough to support us. I thought we would move only a short distance, but when we came across the wheat fields, we had to keep going."

His disgust was obvious, for the land had always belonged to the Maasai and the wildlife, and suddenly the Poor Ones, who cultivate, had taken it over. The thought made him angry again, and Namelok saw the tightening of his jaw muscles in the firelight. He sucked his teeth and let loose a frustrated puff of air. Shaking away his memories, he looked around him and saw where they were, and they both knew that he had to continue with his story, no matter how disturbing and shameful it was.

"We have moved before, that I know, but we always just moved away for a while, from a spot, not from our traditional way of life. Isn't that true?" Just the crackling fire filled the night as Namelok left his question unanswered. "Never before did we move away into a new place where money rules lives and old traditions are forgotten. Do you remember the morning I walked off?"

Was it really only five days ago? Namelok thought to herself. Again she gave no answer.

Reteti rapped his finger against his *oringa*, sending

out a quickening *tap, tap, tap* into the darkness that spilled out of range of the fire's glow. Taking a deep breath, he said, "I could feel all the eyes watching me that morning I left the *enkang*, but I didn't care. I was in a hurry to find a quiet place far from everyone to think and plan for the Council of Elders. I finally sat at the foot of a great old baobab tree, and was almost into a restful nod when I heard shouts. Not too far to the east trotted three *ilmurani*, yelping and laughing as they went."

"So you saw him!" blurted out Namelok.

Her father's head snapped up and he said, "You saw, Namelok-ai? You know what your brother did?"

Namelok nodded her head slowly, never saying a word.

Twitching his shoulders in a quick spasm, he said, "I thought I would be sick as I watched the car full of tourists rush toward my son—my firstborn son—and his friends. It was what I had prayed never to witness, all happening before my eyes."

Namelok sneaked a quick look at her father's face in the flickering firelight, then quickly looked away. His pain was too great to watch as he continued.

Bouncing his *oringa* on the ground faster and faster, it was clear Reteti was forcing himself to continue. "It was more than I could bear, for the warriors began to jump high into the sky, dancing for the tourists. Selling their souls for a few Kenyan *shillingi*." Shaking his head slowly from side to side, he said, "I suddenly realized—it wasn't the tourists' fault. No. The tourists did not force them to dance. The *ilmurani* had offered."

Reteti slunk back down against the tree in the African night. He reached over and picked up a small branch and threw it into the fire. A shower of sparks flew up, and in the sudden burst of light Namelok checked for Siri Aang. She lay by herself at the edge of the bush, so small and alone, it made Namelok's heart ache.

Reteti cleared his throat again and said, "I wanted to cry, for the first time as a grown man. I felt so betrayed by my son that it took my breath away."

His last sentence rested in the cool African night. A dark shape off to the right caught Namelok's attention. She could hear grass being ripped from the ground and finally saw the huge mass of a grazing hippo. She thought about reaching out to her father, but didn't. Instead she said, "Finish the horrible tale, Father. What did you do?"

Reteti rubbed his nose and then pulled on the gray hairs protruding from his chin. He sucked in a breath, then haltingly continued. "After watching Loitipitip standing on the side of the road, posing for his photograph and selling his soul, I questioned Enkai. How could I, a mere man, question her decisions and the turns in life she gives us? I was desperate, shamed that I had not provided for my family's needs or values."

Shaking his head he said, "And so I did something desperate."

THEY SAT SILENTLY for a while, watching the giant hippo graze in the shadows and not looking at each other. Reteti poked the fire again, and a sudden flash of flame sent the hippo off, snorting his displeasure as he heaved his bulk away from the light.

Reteti coughed once and asked, "Do you want to hear more, or is this enough for one night?"

Namelok looked his way and said, "More, *Papa-ai*. I want to hear it all." She picked up a narrow stick and began to pull the thin bark off it. Her eyes constantly checked the edge of the shadows for the little lump of her little sister, Our Secret.

Stretching out his legs and grimacing from moving his swollen heel, he continued. "I didn't stand and shock Loitipitip by my sudden presence. I couldn't face the shame in front of the tourists and guide. I couldn't trust myself to control the rage that was building in my chest. All I knew was that I had to get my family far away from this new place as soon as possible."

Picking up a small piece of firewood, he bounced it in his hand as he said with more force in his voice, "I suddenly knew that I was about to do something that would change my life forever. But why not?! What I had just seen, my son selling his soul, had already done that."

He stopped talking. Taking four deep breaths, he sat straighter and continued. "For three days last month there were two men at the *olduka*, talking, talking, talking. Kakuta had warned us about them, do you remember?"

The flickering firelight reflected off her headpiece as she nodded her head yes. Angrily she said, "I remember you said, 'Not to worry, for we are all Maasai and would never help them.'" She almost regretted it, for she felt her father flinch in shame. But something new inside, some new confidence, wouldn't let her take the words back.

He rushed like a growing dust devil with his story, unable to stop now that he had started. "They were talking to anyone who would listen, barking away with wide arm gestures and foul yellow teeth. I heard the *ilmurani* talking among themselves, about how these men would pay money if someone led them to a rhino.

"The first day the poachers came to the *olduka*, I was as disgusted as all the others. The second day I saw them I thought—just for the passing of a moment—about how maybe I could buy some land so no one could plant on it or ban us from grazing there. I knew exactly where I could go with our family to resume the true, free Maasai life. Then I laughed at myself, because I knew I could no more help these two-legged hyenas than I could give you to an old man to marry."

He blew an explosive puff of air through his tightened lips. "And then on that terrible third day I saw my son selling his photo, and that afternoon I told those disgusting men that I would lead them to the rhinos." He stopped again and sucked his teeth, disgusted with himself. "It's scary how things can change—so fast and so drastically."

Squinting his eyes as a plume of smoke floated his way, Reteti carried on with his story. "After the *ilmurani* left, I went directly to the place the poachers said they would wait. The place they went when everyone chased them from the shop—I never went to the Council of Elders, may Enkai forgive me."

Reteti dropped his head and almost whispered. "They promised me seventy-five thousand *shillingi*. I was sure that could buy someplace where we could be free and live like all the generations before me. They did not tell me why they wanted rhino—I didn't ask. I thought only of getting my family away from this evil place."

He stopped to laugh at himself with derision. "I condemn the young for selling their souls to the tourists and I sold my soul to the poachers. What a sad joke all of this is. Only now am I seeing it. I, who know next to nothing about money, thought I could buy land! And I would buy land that Enkai gave us? Oh, how pitiful."

Shaking his head as if trying to dislodge the realization, he talked again in a voice that sounded as if he too were shocked at what he was hearing. "The poachers and I agreed to meet where the old borehole is, when the sun set. I picked that spot because it was far from everyone, and near some rhino tracks I had seen a few days earlier."

Looking directly at his daughter, he said, "Look at me and tell me you believe me when I say I never saw any baby's prints."

Namelok raised her eyes from the fire and looked at her father. A quick nod was all she could manage.

"If I ever sleep peacefully again, I will be amazed. I met those two as planned, and we drove into the bush. We drove there that night, only four moons past—can that be true? At the very first glimmer of daybreak I found the tracks. I swear that then too I saw no spoor of a baby."

Pulling once again on his beard, he said, "I have to confess, I was in a big hurry to be done with the whole thing, so maybe I didn't look closely enough. My stomach was churning, but I knew it was too late to stop." He cleared his throat and rolled his *oringa* between his two hands. Namelok continued to stare into the fire, sickened and saddened by all she had heard so far, but unable to stop her father's tale.

"I am always impressed by how something so large can move so silently. We came upon the rhino around a large copse. We were surprised by her sudden appearance. She had made no sounds of breaking branches as she walked."

Dropping his eyes to his hands that spun his *oringa* back and forth, as if he were trying to start a fire, he avoided looking again at his daughter. He heaved a sigh of shame. "The big mother was in front, and her baby must have been walking behind, hidden, for I didn't see it. The mother charged at the men, who walked to my right, and I hoped in my darkest heart that she would get one of them. Run her horn right through the fat man's belly, or trample the fool in the floppy hat. But she never had a chance. They hit her again and again with rifle shots that repeated as fast as a woodpecker hammering."

Reteti glanced quickly at Namelok and saw a stream of tears running down her face. A small sob escaped him at the sight of his daughter's pain. Words poured from his mouth that he could not stop. "The mother rhino ran a few more steps after being shot again and again, before she crashed to the ground. My whole body shook as each bullet hit her, and I looked inward and shuddered. The men were laughing and hooting and celebrating the kill. I only wanted to run. When they began hacking off the horn with a *panga*, I turned and vomited."

He stopped, clearly overwhelmed by his own words and memories. With a catch in his voice he continued. "The fat one said, 'Old woman, don't you like money?' First he pointed the horn at me, then he held the horn high, bragging, 'Oh, yes. *Bwana* Johnson will pay a lot of money for this.' He laughed like a hyena and I retched again." The memory ran through Reteti's mind clearly, Namelok could see it, and he shook his head hard, trying to get rid of it.

He plunged on with his story in the darkness. He spoke quickly, as if he had no control over his words. "I wanted to run, but I couldn't because I needed to be paid. I had just betrayed this beautiful animal for money, and so if I didn't get the money, it would have died for nothing.

"Don't you see, My Sweetest One? I wanted the money to set my family free. I needed to think about that. To remember that that was why I was there. I had a son posing for pictures and a daughter who wanted to delay her *emuratare* and go to school. Both things are so distant from a true Maasai's life or mind. These are the things that drove me to a terrible and shameful act."

He looked over at her, to see if she would respond to that. But instead Namelok sat silently, tears running down her face. He saw her look at Siri Aang, whose little body rested just beyond the flickering light of the flames. Namelok purred "currrr, currrr" to the baby rhino, connecting herself to Our Secret as her father's awful story filled her head. She couldn't deny to herself in that moment that she had been a big part of her father's problem, but she still couldn't forgive him just yet. All the while the call of a nightjar rang out, *chucker chucker, chucker chucker.*

Forcing himself to continue, Reteti picked up his fly whisk, which was resting in his lap. "I turned my back to the carnage and told myself, 'Stay focused like the young *ilmurani* hunting the lion.' I sent my gaze wandering and spotted an elegant giraffe, walking along the horizon like a strolling shadow. The sun had just risen from the flat plains stretched far behind the large giraffe, creating a stark silhouette."

Closing his eyes, he said, "I remember soaking up the sight, and saying aloud, 'Beauty. Life,' telling myself that this horrible, needless death I was involved in was the exception, not the way my life has always been.

"Then I told myself, it isn't needless, for when I receive the money for this horrible deed, I will buy cows—not land—and grain for our family. We shall head toward the far side of the Mara River where few people go and we will be free, and my children shall be true Maasai once again."

He flicked his fly whisk from side to side, watching it with an intensity it didn't deserve. "I kept telling myself this as I continued to stare at the giraffe. Its long neck bobbed with each step, and those long legs seemed to make a fleeting frame around the rising sun. I thought again of that terrible day when I saw Loitipitip posing on the roadside, and that made me sicker than the dead rhino."

Looking straight at his silent, weeping daughter, Reteti said with added force in his voice, "I turned back to the carnage with renewed conviction in my decision, My Sweetest One. Then even that new conviction faltered at the sight I saw. It's difficult to say which was more repulsive, the butchered rhino's face or the laughing men covered in blood." A shiver ran down his spine and he paused to catch his breath.

"There was Mwangi, who had smatterings of horn and bone on him, and his fat friend wore a splotchy cloak of blood. Mwangi held the biggest horn high. He did a little dance about all the money he would get. I felt sickened again, and told them, 'Stop the foolishness, we must leave.'

"As we marched back to the vehicle, I knew I could not get into it with them. Their stench and joy and total lack of respect for this animal left me feeling empty and sick and disgusted with myself."

He paused again, unable to lift his head and face to the daughter who had survived days alone in the bush. The daughter who had risked her life for the things he had trained her to believe in. His voice dropped to a whisper as he said, "I hate myself for what I have done, and feel great shame for my actions."

32

IN THE LIGHT of the fire surrounded by a huge dark-ness, Namelok spoke for the second time since he had started his story. "How did you find Siri Aang?"

"I first saw her after the poachers were finished. She was hiding in the bush, not far from where we first saw the mother. They were so foolishly happy with the mother's horns that they didn't notice the baby. They paid me this. I have not looked at it. I just took it so I would never have to see them again."

He pulled a large wad of *shillingi* from beneath a fold of cloth resting over his belt. He dropped it to the ground as if he couldn't stand the touch of it. They both left it there.

"I said I would walk back, for they made me sick and I made me sick. As the younger one turned to get into the car, he caught a glimpse of the baby rhino trotting away. He raised his gun to shoot it, so I hit his arm with my *oringa*. He wanted to shoot me, but Mwangi said, 'Don't shoot him. We don't need any curious rangers who might hear the shots asking us anything.'

"I didn't trust them, so I ran after the baby, to scare it away." Reteti looked at his foot where the thorn had been and gave a short laugh. "It was longer than I can say—a distance meant more for a young warrior to run than an old man like myself, I crashed behind the baby through the bush. That is when I stepped on the thorn. I stopped suddenly, and so did the tired little rhino. I collapsed to the ground, and so did she. And so we stayed together, but apart. She walks slowly and so do I. One day she led me to water. And each day we browsed in an acacia copse."

He gazed over at the little rhino, barely visible in the firelight. "I could never figure out why she tolerated my scent, but now I know. She had had human contact long before we met." His eyes finally rested again on his daughter, but she wasn't looking at him. She was staring at the little rhino, who was squealing softly in her sleep.

"Currrr, currrr," she called out to calm Siri Aang.

"I am ashamed for betraying Enkai, who made us the friend and protector of all wildlife, and the rhino, which never did me any harm." Then he sat forward from the tree trunk he was leaning against. "But a man must do what he must do to protect his family too. I wanted to protect mine from something too difficult to contemplate—losing who and what they are." She felt him shift again, unable to rise and walk because of his injured foot.

Reteti gazed off into the African night. The power of the moon's glow bathed a herd of zebra in a golden light. Bouncing his *oringa* on the hard ground, he said, "Now how can I face the family with the shame I bear?" She could feel his eyes begging her to look at him, and when she did, he asked, "How can I gain the trust and respect and love again of My Sweetest One?"

Namelok didn't answer right away. The sound of crickets hummed along, as she watched the grazing herd of zebra slowly passing by their camp in the moonlight. Finally looking directly at her father, she said, "There is something you can do. I must tell you I swore to Siri Aang's little tracks, and to the corpse of her mother, that I would find the poachers and turn them over to Kakuta. Who is *Bwana* Johnson?"

"The man who sent them out here to hunt the rhino. The one who will buy the horns."

"To help me keep my promise, Father, you must tell Kakuta about all these men."

His voice shook with frustration as he asked, "How can I do that? Then all will know what I have done, and that is a shame I cannot bear. It is a pity I did not think of this shame before I acted."

Shaking her head from side to side, and staring at Siri Aang as both she and the baby rhino rose, Namelok puffed out a breath of air. "I don't know, Father. I don't know, but I have a promise to keep to Siri Aang. Let's think about it all later," she said as she stoked the fire. "Now one of us should sleep, and one keep the fire big. I would not mind a short rest," she said, looking down at him when he made no reply.

"Fine," he finally answered, "for I am not ready for sleep. There is still much to think about."

Lying down for the first time in three days, her back against her father's legs extended straight out in front of him, Namelok felt exhausted and safe. The night chatter of owls and crickets and the soft sound of Siri Aang pulling branches from the bushes pushed her toward sleep. Just before drifting off, she said ever so softly, "Think about what we shall do with Siri Aang. If you think that now that I have found her again, alive, that I will just leave her, you are wrong, Father." And with that little threat she fell into a welcome slumber.

NAMELOK HAD BEEN awake for hours when the sun's first golden light arced across the horizon. As the flattened moon moved toward the land, in her mind she heard again and again her father's story. Her emotions raced from anger to disgust to sadness to pride. She felt an overwhelming sense of exhaustion, but not from a lack of sleep. She didn't realize she was speaking out loud until her father answered her question, "How did life get so hard?"

"You are not the first to ask that," he said in a husky voice. "I have asked it more times in the last six days than I have in the last five months. That is something I did not think was possible."

"And do you have an answer?"

He shook his head, his empty ear flaps dangling back and forth. "I have tried to blame everyone, from Enkai to you, but I know where I should look." He examined his own hands and legs, then smacked his chest with a flat open hand, a *thump, thump, thump* filling the air. "Here," he said. "Here is where I should look."

Namelok stirred the fire, for she didn't want it to go out. "You have time," she said. "We will spend the day here, for you need to stay off that foot. If Siri Aang wanders, I will follow her and bring her back." They both looked over to where the baby rhino was once again browsing.

Siri Aang looked helpless without her powerful mother at her side. Namelok noticed how her two stubby horns were beginning to take real shape, and shuddered at the thought of what troubles they could bring the rhino one day. "Look into yourself, *Papa-ai*, and ask Enkai for the answer of what shall become of this motherless baby rhino. How long did you plan to follow Siri Aang?" she asked. "You were following her, weren't you? Not chasing her?"

"Yes," he answered, "I was following her. I felt a responsibility for her, and a total loss for what I could do for her but follow and hope no predator came her way."

Looking at the baby rhino, he said, "I had no plan, and I still don't know what we can do."

Namelok stood suddenly and began pulling fresh strips of bark off the tree's trunk. She put one piece into her mouth and chewed it with quick little bites. She looked at the four-month-old rhino and asked her father, "Would you like to know Siri Aang's and my history?"

"Do you tell me to shame me?" he asked.

She was insulted by the question. "How could you ask such a thing? I only want to tell you so that you'll know how I won't just leave her here."

He patted the ground beside him for her to sit down. "My Sweetest One, please tell me your story."

Carrying the little pile of fresh bark over to her father, she handed it to him, then settled on the ground.

She sat with a single smooth motion, picked up the stick she used to poke the fire with and recognized it as the black one she had picked up on the plain. The same stick that had helped her father walk now helped keep their fire alive.

She smoothed the red and white cloth she wore across her legs. It was so dirty. Then she rearranged her necklaces until they felt right. She patted her headband and twisted her earrings as she gathered her thoughts. Turning to look at her father, she found his full gaze upon her, ready to listen.

"*Papa-ai*, do you know a thick copse directly north of the *enkang*? It stands a bit far from the camp; in fact there are two smaller copses before you reach it." She could see he was ready to reprimand her for going so far, alone and only for wood, so she sped up.

"I found it by accident one day, when I could no longer take the raised voices in the *enkang* about how bad our life had become. I needed to get away and used collecting firewood as my excuse. I found this copse, with great piles of fallen branches, an endless supply of firewood. I knew that if no one visited it, I would have a supply for a long time."

Looking at her father, she said, "And I also knew that I had found a haven, for the only voices there were those of the go-away bird, the crickets, the cooing doves and my own. I could have conversations of one with total freedom."

Poking at the fire, she leaned forward to turn a large, slow-burning log on it, then jumped up and started walking as she talked. "One day I had my most incredible experience. As I collected wood and laughed aloud at something funny I had said, all the cicadas suddenly went very quiet."

Gazing over at Our Secret, who was once again resting in the very early light, Namelok smiled. "I stopped and looked all around me when I noticed the sudden quiet. First across the plains to the north and south and west, and then finally deep into the copse. As my eyes adjusted to the criss-crossed branches, I suddenly saw a large black shape. Our distance was not so great, but the mosaic of branches crossing each other again and again built a wall between us. At first my fear was great. Then I realized what I was seeing—a black rhino giving birth."

She looked down at Reteti. "I thought of you, Father, and the ways you help new calves into this world. I whispered to the mother rhino, telling her, 'Push harder, push harder.' She didn't run and she didn't charge, she just got ready to give birth.

"Do you understand, Father? I was there at Siri Aang's birth. I loved the new baby rhino as soon as she stood, only minutes after being born, wobbly and wet and the perfect copy of her mother. From someplace deep inside I made the 'currrr, currrr' sound, and she looked my way and we were connected."

Namelok walked back and forth between her father and Siri Aang, gently bouncing her fists on her thighs. "For the first week after she was born I made sure to visit them every day. I always approached with the soft 'currrr, currrr' to let them know it was me that was coming. *Yieyio* Emuny Narok never once ran from me, nor hid her baby from me, for she knew I meant them no harm."

The words brought a taste of bitterness to her mouth as she suddenly remembered where they were and why. "Siri Aang and her mother and I were a family. I always promised them that they were safe with my big family, the Maasai, because we are the protectors and friends of all Enkai's animals."

Namelok choked, swallowing a gasp, while sudden tears flowed freely. With a ravaged face she turned to her father and asked, "Do you remember the last time you told Loitipitip and me the story '*Inkishu*—Enkai's Greatest Gift'?" He nodded yes, and the look of remorse in his eyes made her stop the words spilling from her mouth.

She took a long deep breath to slow down the angry words that were tumbling out. "When the rhinos began to disappear for days at a time, I was worried. Then I finally figured out that they were going to the river to drink and wallow. Time was passing so quickly, and Our Secret was growing up."

She took another very deep breath and said, "*Papa-ai*, you are not the only one who has things to be ashamed of. I have told many lies over the past four months. Lies like I never told before."

She looked off to the horizon as her voice floated on the warming morning air. "I hid my bleeding for three months before Mother discovered it."

She felt her father's head snap up and his eyes lock

on her when she said this. "At first I wanted to go to school only to delay *emuratare* because I knew I would lose contact with the rhinos. I was sure that the four months of recovery would make me lose my rhino family."

Namelok snorted as she told her own sad story. "Then I heard the radio program and my mind started saying, 'Why should I do this at all?'"

She tapped her hands on her thighs as she paced back and forth in front of her father. "I started lying so I could visit the rhinos every day."

Namelok could feel her father's steely gaze upon her. He didn't say a word, just as she had stayed silent the night before as he talked. She finally looked into his eyes and took a deep breath. "I am sure they will tell you what I did the day before you left, so I will tell you myself. I asked Mother in front of all the other women and girls why I had to rush into *emuratare* and marriage." Her father's eyes narrowed in a shocked squint as she said this.

A dark frown flashed across his face and he asked, "Is that why everyone acted like restless cattle that night? Is that why your mother insisted that we do the ceremony in four weeks' time?"

Namelok nodded her head and said, "*Aaa*. I knew later that I should not have spoken in public, for this is a matter for mother and daughter to discuss." She kicked the ground as she said, "I decided that I will follow tradition when we get back, for my mother, for my family, but I will not force my future daughters to do this. But that, Father, is something so far in the future that we need not worry about it now."

Her father coughed and asked her, "What were you running away from—the *emuratare* and marriage? I cannot believe that, for no child of mine, male or female, is a coward."

Blowing out a long noisy breath, she looked once again at Siri Aang. "I am afraid that that is what people will think, but that has nothing to do with why I am here. I promised Mother I would be initiated, and I shall."

Namelok stared at Siri Aang as the baby rhino struggled to her feet. The sun had risen high in the sky, sending down a building heat. "I am here because of the rhinos. Mother had told me of my *emuratare* date so each day I was more desperate to spend time with *Yieyio* Emuny Narok and Siri Aang. With my rhino family."

Namelok looked at her father again. "But for two days, after you had left for the Council of Elders, I had not seen the rhinos. On the third day as I looked about and wondered what to do, I saw the vultures. They led me to *Yieyio* Emuny Narok. And like you, Father, I retched. Then I cried, and then I got very angry. And that was when I started following the tracks that led me to Siri Aang and you." She sat down wearily, leaning against the trunk of the tree next to him. Telling her story had worn her out, and her father gently put his hand over hers that lay on the ground.

"We won't leave her, your Siri Aang," he said, "but I don't know what we can do with her. We can't spend the rest of our days following her until she's big enough to defend herself." He saw the alarm that crossed My Sweetest One's face and spoke quickly to reassure her. "Why don't you rest? I will let you know if she moves from sight, but now with the sun nearing its apex she will stay in the shade, and rest too. And while you rest, I'll try to think of what we can do."

The day passed quietly. Neither one felt the need for talk, for each had much to think about. Namelok could tell that the day's rest was good for her, and for her father as well when she changed the sap dressing on his injured foot. The red streak had already disappeared, and the skin was not stretched so tightly.

As the sun dipped toward the western horizon, Namelok gathered a large pile of wood to burn gently in the huge African night. She also broke off two small sticks from the empty branch of berries, gave one to her father and put one into her mouth. They both chewed quietly on the end of their sticks, making a flared fiber to rub their teeth with. At sunset a flock of egrets flew overhead, their white underbodies reflecting the oranges and pinks of the sunset. A large herd of wildebeest grazed in the distance, and the moon rose late. The fire burned low, sending out only a small amount of light.

chapter

34

THEY BOTH WATCHED the fire and listened to a herd of
zebra barking in the distance, beyond the fire's light.
When the moon was at its highest point, spilling down
a bright white light, there came a loud snort from the
shadows. Siri Aang jumped to her feet and trotted with
quick little steps, back and forth. Reteti held out his arm
to stop his daughter from rising. A strange squealing
sound came from Our Secret as she continued to pace
back and forth. A high-pitched mewing flew back
through the night air, and the little rhino's ears shot up.
Namelok made a move to stand, but her father held her
down. She glared at him, and he said, "I know the sound.
Trust me, we must not interfere."

Siri Aang held her nose high, sniffing the air in all
directions. Slowly she walked toward the darkness. As
she entered into the area not covered by the tree's widespread moon shadow, a large figure moved into view. Its
head was held high, sniffing away. Two big horns stuck
out from the face, and it walked with a slow, measured
pace. A hoarse sound, like a man clearing his throat,
filled the air from the big rhino.

With tentative steps, the big black rhino approached
Siri Aang. She walked around the baby as it released a

high squeal, the call of a baby to a mother. Enkai must have been present, for the human scent and smell of smoke was hidden as the wind blew from behind the big animal.

Namelok's smile was bright in the moonlight. She could see her father was just as pleased to see the big rhino sniff the baby, then give her a nudge with her head. Siri Aang leaned into the nudge, and would have stayed there indefinitely if another baby, just about her size, hadn't appeared from behind its mother. It held its head high as it sniffed the air. The two young ones looked at each other, and then stood close.

"A new family," whispered Namelok. "Good-bye, my friend," she said a little louder as the three rhinos moved out of view and into the darkness. Tears streamed down her face and splashed onto her father's hand. She didn't know when it had happened, but the restraining arm had turned into a tight handhold, and she squeezed back. She could not remember the last time she had really held her father's hand.

"You saved her," Namelok said.

"And you saved me. I will talk to Kakuta, and give him this money that feels so filthy. And face my shame."

Namelok stroked his hand and said, "*Papa-ai*, I must tell you something. I know now that Loitipitip was also desperate, for your sadness was more than he could bear. He told me his age-mates had given him an idea to help. Last night after we talked, I realized that that was why he was posing to sell his photo. He was trying to earn money for you. He told me he had a plan but never said what it was."

Raising her eyes from their entwined hands, she said, "And I want to go to school, *Papa-ai*, for more than just a way to delay my *emuratare*. I want to stop the shop-keeper who steals money from people who can't add and subtract."

Her father's head popped up and he said, "He cheats us?"

Namelok nodded yes. "Us and every other Maasai who doesn't count. Joseph the teacher showed me that one day." Carefully she pulled her folded treasure from her waistline. Spreading the paper on the ground she said, "Look, *Papa-ai*. It's my name." She ran her finger under the letters. "It says Namelok."

She doodled in the dirt like the students she had watched. "Changes are coming, Father."

Namelok heard her words before she really thought about them. "Father, isn't it better to be part of the changes happening than to just be victims of it all?"

Then, quickly she said, "*Papa-ai*, will you really go to Kakuta? I am sure that we can do it so no one will know. Just tell him what you have told me. Give him the names of the poachers and the man who sent them. Then he can find them all."

With a quick laugh she said, "And when the family and friends ask where we have been, we will say, 'In the bush,' but nothing more. If they want to believe that I ran from my *emuratare* and you came looking for me, that is fine." Nodding her head to the flames, she said, "*Aaa*, that is fine."

Then with a wide smile she said, "Not to worry, *Papa-ai*, for all this," and she swung her arms wide to include the tree they slept beneath, the direction the rhinos had gone, the wide African night that embraced them, "all of this shall always be *siri aang*. Our secret."

Author's Note:

I FIRST CAME in contact with the Maasai in 1975, as a Peace Corps volunteer in Kenya. They dazzled me with their elegance, style and pride. Over the nineteen years I spent in Africa, I visited Kenya over and over, each time becoming more aware of the changes facing the Maasai culture, much like other nomadic tribes of Africa. Suddenly young warriors were stopping tourist vehicles to pose for photos, villages were popping up on the out-skirts of national parks for tours, and villages were becoming permanent.

Many different factors contributed to these changes, such as the start of government controls, natural disas-ters changing the landscape, and increased population pressure turning traditionally open fields into cultivated zones. It was clear to me that the Maasai, just like the Tuareg of Niger, the San of southern Africa, and the Wodabbe of West Africa, all nomadic cultures, were being forced to change and settle.

To write this book, I depended on a good Maasai friend, Kakuta Ole Maimai Hamisi. He made sure that all my cultural descriptions were accurate, and assured me that the basic premise of young people wanting to study as many adults resisted the variety of changes being forced upon them, is, in fact, true. At one point, Kakuta and I sat on St. John for a week and discussed his youth, Maasai traditions, the current challenges facing his culture, and his efforts to help the Maasai make changes while maintaining their rich cultural heritage. He also gave me his grandfather's own words for the chapter under the tree when Namelok's father tells the stranger what he thinks about the changes being forced upon the Maasai.

This book was written for the same reason I wrote *One Night*: to document another culture before it totally changes from nomadic to sedentary.

Namelok's encounters with wildlife are based on my own journal entries and experiences in the bush of Africa over nineteen years.

Namelok (Nah-may-**lock**)   Main character, a twelve-year-old Maasai girl. Means "Sweetest One."

Emuny Narok (Eh-moonie Nah-rock)   *Emuny* is "rhino" and *Narok* is "black."

Namelok-ai (Nah-may-**lockeye**)   *Ai* means "my," so together it means "My Sweetest One."

Nasieku (Nah-see-ay**ku**)   Third wife of Namelok's father.

Yieyio Emuny Narok (Yeh-yo)   Means "mother," so "Mother Black Rhino."

Siri Aang (Serie Ong)   "Our Secret," the new baby rhino.

Reteti (Reh-te-tee)   Namelok's father. His name means "The Helpful One" from a powerful tree, similar to the acacia tree, used for medicines, called the Oreteti.

Nanana-ai (Nah-nah-**naheye**)   First wife, whose name means "My Fruitful One."

Namunyak-ai (Nah-mon-**yakeye**)   Namelok's mother. It means "My Luckiest One."

Saitoti (Sigh-toe-tee)   A rare Maasai name with no meaning, just like Kakuta.

Loitipitip (Loy-tip-ee-tip)   Namelok's oldest half brother. His name literally means "The Drizzle One," for someone born during a rain. His name is actually taken from Oloitipitip, the first Maasai politician and member of parliament. He died mysteriously in 1982.

Lankat (Lan-**kot**)   Namelok's sister, a little more than one year younger than her. No meaning for her name.

Enkai (En-**kai**)   The Maasai god. The Maasai believe that God is a woman. She is greatly revered.

Sambeke (Sam-**beh**-ke)   Namelok's half brother. No meaning for the name.

Nosiligi (No-sil-li-**gee**)   Means a baby of hope as a new way of life progresses. Her name means literally "Born in a Time of Change."

Papa-ai (Pa-**pah**eye)   My father.

Kakuta (Kah-ku-tah)   Traditional name of the Maasai park ranger also called Stephen.

Maasinta (Maa-sin-tah)   Main character in folktale of "Enkai's Greatest Gift," the story of the creation of cattle and how all were given to Maasai. He is the father of all Maasai.

Oltorroboni (Ol-tow-**row**-bonnie)   Servant of Maasinta.

Loibon Saidimu (Loy-bon Sigh-dee-moo)   A *loibon* is a respected holy man and healer. *Saidimu* means "The Capable One."

Mwangi (Mwang-ee)   A man's name from a different tribe. It is instantly recognizable to all Maasai as someone from town, not a Maasai.

Aaa (Ahh)   Yes.

Ashe (Ah-**shay**)   Thank you.

Bwana (Bwah-nah)   Swahili for "mister" or "boss."

Emuratare (Em-you-rah-ta-**ray**)   The circumcision ceremony that turns a young girl into a woman. Also the point when a young girl loses her freedom to visit the warriors and wander on her own.

Endorko (En-door-**koh**)   A tree that has heart-shaped leaves and is used for starting fires. The match tree.

Enkang (En-**kang**)   A circular enclosure where family and livestock live. The wall is made of four types of thorn trees.

Enkosikos (In-**koh**-see-kos)   A squash popular with herders.

Entasupa. Kasidan inkera (En-ta-sue-**pa**. Ka-see-**dan** in-ker-a)   Are the children well?

Enyoore (En-yo-o-**ray**)   A tool made from a dried, thick branch of the *endorko* tree. It is split in half and laid open to provide the friction point for starting a fire.

Esosian (Eh-so-see-**an**)   A tool for cleaning out milk gourds. It's a stick with a bent end and a tuft of separated fibers on the end, making a brush. Used to rub burning coals around inside the gourd to kill bacteria.

Eunoto (You-no-**toe**)   The ceremony for a warrior to become a Junior Elder. The mother of the warrior shaves his long braids off as part of the ceremony.

Ilmeuti (Ill-may-uo-tee)   Giraffes. "Il" prefix always signifies plural of word that follows.

Ilmurani (Il-mur-ra-**ni**)   Warriors. The warrior age group of young men, anywhere from ten to eighteen years of age.

Imasaa (Ee-maa-**sa**)   Jewelry made for brides by all women friends and relatives.

Inkishu (In-key-**shoe**)   Cattle.

Irmankula (Ir-**man**-koo-**lah**)   A very sweet berry that can also cause thirst. The branches from this shrub are used for toothbrush sticks.

Iseuri (Ee-say-ur-ree)   The name of an older age group, which means "During a fruitful green season." This group of elders are also known for their fighting ability.

Isiruai (I-si-roo-**eye**)   Eland.

Kasidan inkishu (Ka-see-**dan** in-kee-shu)   Are the cattle well?

Kikoy (Key-koy)   A Swahili word meaning a colorful cloth worn by women for a skirt or cover.

Kokooo (Koh-kooo)   Grandmother.

Kuyiaa (Koo-yeh-ah)   Grandfather.

Maa (Mah)   The official language spoken by Maasai.

Maasai (Mah-sigh)   The nomadic pastoralists of

Kenya and Tanzania. They are known for their connection to their surroundings and believe that they rightfully own all cattle on earth.

Manyatta (Man-yah-tah)   Same as *enkang*, but usually refers to where the warriors live.

Mzee (Mmm-zay)   Swahili for "old man." Usually used as a sign of respect.

Olchurai (Ol-chu-**rye**)   A type of acacia tree that all Maasai know. During the drought season, they chew the bark to kill thirst. Also used in soup to help digestion.

Olduka (Ol-due-**kah**)   A shop or small store.

Olesere (Oh-leh-se-**ray**)   Good-bye.

Olmurani (Ol-mur-ra-**ni**)   Singular for *warrior*. "Ol" prefix always denotes "one."

Oloirien (Oh-loy-ree-**in**)   A dark olive wood used to clean out milk gourds. The end is burned and the live charcoals are dropped into the gourd.

Olpirun (Ol-pee-**roan**)   A slender, straight branch also from the *endorko* tree that is rolled rapidly between the palms of the hands against the flat surface of the *enyoore*. The heat and friction eventually produce a spark to start a fire.

Oringa (Oh-ring-ah) A stick carried by all Elders, often called an authority stick.

Panga (Pan-**gah**)   Like a machete, used for cutting wood, clearing bush, etc.

Shillingi (Sh-li-ing-**ee**)   Swahili word for shilling, the money of Kenya.

Shuka (Shoe-**kah**)   A red robe worn draped over one or two shoulders by both men and women, similar to a toga.

Supa! (Sue-**pa!**)   Greeting of hello.

This glossary is spelled phonetically for easier pronunciation. The bold indicates where the accent falls. This has not been compiled by a linguist, but by a Maa native speaker.